PUPPY IN A PUDDLE

A puppy was sitting in a shallow puddle just to the right of Mandy's bare feet. She looked down at its little face and tangled, shaggy coat. She took the little dog gently in her arms. Its feet scrambled with fear as Mandy picked it up. Then, feeling the warmth of her arms, it began to relax against her. The puppy snuggled closer, shivering, and gave a tiny whimper.

"Oh!" Mandy said softly. "Oh, you poor little thing. What are you doing here?"

Give someone you love a home!
Read about the animals of Animal Ark™

PUPPY
in a PUDDLE

Ben M. Baglio

Illustrations by Ann Baum

Cover illustration by
Pete Mueller

AN
APPLE
PAPERBACK

SCHOLASTIC INC.
New York Toronto London Auckland Sydney
Mexico City New Delhi Hong Kong Buenos Aires

ISBN 0-439-34389-5

12 11 10 9 8 7 6 5 4 3   2 3 4 5 6 7/0

Printed in the U.S.A.   40
First Scholastic printing, January 2002

To my best friend, Tristan Chapman,
and to Hugo, his wonderful, big puppy

Special thanks to Ingrid Hoare
Thanks also to C. J. Hall,
B.Vet.Med., M.R.C.V.S., for reviewing
the veterinary information contained in this book

One

"What *is* that smell?" asked Mandy Hope as she walked through the door from her home into the reception area of Animal Ark. She wrinkled her nose. "It smells like a beauty salon in here!"

Jean Knox, the clinic receptionist, put a finger to her lips. Then she chuckled. "It's Toby. I think Mrs. Ponsonby has drenched him in her perfume. Apparently, he found something nasty to roll in — and came home smelling bad enough to cause Pandora to have a fit!"

"Oh, no!" Mandy said, grinning. Everyone in Welford knew how Mrs. Ponsonby acted when it came to the little Pekingese. "Not a real fit?" she whispered.

1

Jean nodded. She put on her glasses and went back to the paperwork on her desk.

Mandy looked over the counter to where Mrs. Ponsonby was sitting in the clinic waiting room. Apart from the stout, nicely dressed lady and her two dogs, the waiting room was empty. The clinic was unusually quiet for a Saturday morning.

Mrs. Ponsonby was holding a lace-edged handkerchief under her nose with one hand and holding her scruffy mongrel pup, Toby, on the leash with the other. Pandora, the Pekingese, sat on Mrs. Ponsonby's lap, her long cream-colored fur spread out over her owner's flowery dress. The spoiled little dog looked calm and untroubled.

"Hello, Mrs. Ponsonby," Mandy called.

"Mandy, dear!" breathed Mrs. Ponsonby, looking up. "Do you have any idea just how much longer your father is likely to be? I think this is an emergency visit."

"He's in the middle of an operation, Mrs. Ponsonby, but Dr. Emily shouldn't be much longer," Jean called. "And there's no one ahead of you, so you should be able to go right in, in a minute or two."

"Yes," Mandy said reassuringly. "It's really quiet for a Saturday morning clinic."

She slipped out from behind the reception desk and went to say hello to Toby and Pandora. "What's Pandora's problem, Mrs. Ponsonby?" she asked.

"Well," said Mrs. Ponsonby, looking pained, "Toby arrived in the kitchen this morning reeking of something foul, which upset poor Pandora. I'm certain she had a fit of some kind. She was panting, and her eyes were bulging — it was awful. And then I decided to disguise the dreadful smell with some perfume, but I splashed it in Toby's eye and he gave such a terrible yell."

Mandy noticed that one of Toby's eyes was half-closed, but he seemed to be in his usual high spirits. He wagged his tail happily at Mandy. She stroked his head. The scent of lavender, mingling with the more pungent stench that Toby had so happily rolled in, rose into the air. Mandy coughed. "Don't worry, Toby," she said. "We'll have you back to normal in no time. Both of you," she added, smiling at Pandora. "Sounds like you've had a bad morning, Mrs. Ponsonby."

"I have, dear," Mrs. Ponsonby sighed.

As Mandy was petting Toby, the door of one of the examination rooms opened. She turned around and saw her mother washing her hands at the sink. A man holding a cat in a wicker basket was just leaving the exam room. "Thanks so much," he said. "I'll bring Cassie back in a day or two. Good-bye."

"Bye," said Dr. Emily, drying her hands on a small towel. Toby yapped sharply as the cat let out a mournful wail.

Mandy's mother waved at her through the open door of the exam room, then spotted Mrs. Ponsonby, who was struggling to stand up with Pandora in her arms.

"Hello, Mrs. Ponsonby," Dr. Emily called cheerfully, tucking a few strands of her long red hair behind her ear. "Come on in. Oh . . . both of them today?" She winked at Mandy, then closed the door.

Jean caught Mandy's eye and they laughed. Mandy wandered over to the window. It was a hot June day, and the green hills beyond the town looked inviting in the sunshine. *It won't be long until the start of summer vacation*, she thought happily. There would be lots of opportunities to help out at Animal Ark once school was finished, and hours of exploring the hills around Welford with her best friend James Hunter and his Labrador, Blackie.

"Ah, here comes a patient!" Mandy told Jean, who was busy with some paperwork. Mandy went to open the clinic door for a visitor she hadn't seen before. He was a tall, tan man dressed in a blue denim shirt and jeans, and carrying a large cardboard box against his chest. He smiled as Mandy stood aside to let him in.

"Mr. Taylor," he told Jean, propping the edge of the box on the counter. "And this is Rush. He's come for his twelve-week vaccination."

"Hello," Jean smiled. "Would you just fill out this card for me, please, Mr. Taylor? Dr. Adam is just finishing a small operation. We won't keep you long."

"May I see Rush?" Mandy asked Mr. Taylor, pointing to the box.

"Sure." Mr. Taylor set the box down on the floor and lifted the flaps. Then he went back to his card.

Mandy bent down to look inside. Two pink-rimmed blue eyes looked up at her from behind a long fringe of fluffy white fur. A small, black, buttonlike nose twitched with interest. "Oh!" she exclaimed. "He's gorgeous!"

"He's an Old English sheepdog puppy," Mr. Taylor told her with pride, handing the completed card to Jean. "They were used for moving livestock to market," Mr. Taylor told her. "The dog's hair was clipped along with the sheep and the hair was woven to make blankets. Did you know that?"

"No, I didn't," Mandy said. "I can't imagine him herding sheep!" She grinned. "Hello, Rush." Captivated, she gently stroked the puppy's little head. "Aren't you a sweetie?" Rush wagged his stump of a tail and the back end of his body wagged with it. He toppled over comically inside the box, then put both paws on the rim in an effort to get out and climb into Mandy's arms.

"Oh, no you don't," said Mr. Taylor, easing him back.

"Mr. Taylor and . . . Rush," called Dr. Adam from the doorway of the exam room. Mandy looked up at her father and smiled.

"Mr. Taylor has an Old English sheepdog pup, Dad," she told him. "Can I watch while he has his injection, please?"

"If Mr. Taylor doesn't mind." He smiled and turned to speak to the puppy's owner. "My daughter wants to be a

vet, Mr. Taylor," Dr. Adam told his client. "Just like her parents."

Mr. Taylor readily agreed that Mandy could watch, and carried Rush into the exam room. The puppy sat in the box, his furry head just showing over the cardboard rim, peering around uneasily. He sniffed. There was an assortment of confusing smells in the room: disinfectant, medicines, the lingering smell of strong perfume — and other animals. Rush whimpered.

"Put him on the table, please," Dr. Adam said. "Now, let's have a look at you, little fellow." He lifted Rush gently out of the box. The puppy's feet slid out from under him on the slippery surface of the metal counter and Mandy instinctively reached out to stroke and comfort the nervous little dog. She watched her father as he examined Rush, applying gentle pressure to the puppy's abdomen, looking into each ear and opening his mouth to check his teeth and gums.

"Rush is due for his twelve-week vaccination, right, Mr. Taylor?" he asked. Mandy saw that her father was frowning.

"Yes, he's just twelve weeks now," said Mr. Taylor. He did a quick mental calculation. "Yes, that's right. We bought him when he was eight weeks old." He nodded with certainty.

Mandy was still playing with the puppy, who now seemed at ease. He peeped out over the crook of her suntanned elbow and blinked.

"Strange," murmured Dr. Adam, opening Rush's mouth a second time. "He looks younger than twelve weeks. Of course, he could just be a late developer, but it's unusual."

"Where did you get him?" Mandy asked, half wishing she could have a puppy herself.

"I bought him from a breeder on the road to Walton," Mr. Taylor replied. "Mrs. Merrick."

"Oh, yes," said Dr. Adam. "I know of her, but we haven't met. Katharine Merrick. She has a good reputation." He frowned as he put his stethoscope on Rush's chest. "He seems in good shape — but I'm going to hold off giving him that shot today, Mr. Taylor. I'm sure that he's still too young for the vaccination."

"Really? Well, should I come back in another couple of weeks?" Mr. Taylor asked, while Mandy stroked the puppy. Rush licked her cheek with a tiny pink tongue.

"Yes, if you don't mind. I'll give you a wormer for him." Dr. Adam turned away and rummaged through a cabinet on the far side of the small room. He came back to the table. He was writing out the instructions on the packet of worming medicine when his stethoscope slipped from around his neck. It clattered loudly on to the table behind Rush. Mandy jumped. "Dad!"

"Sorry, love," said Dr. Adam. He frowned. "Now, that is odd."

"Odd?" asked Mr. Taylor. "What's odd?"

"Well," began Dr. Adam, "Rush didn't react at all to that loud noise just behind him. It was as though he didn't hear a thing . . . Mandy, distract him by playing with him for a minute, will you?"

Mandy leaned forward and blew gently on the puppy's face. Rush sneezed and shook his head, then began to chew on her fingers, making a small growling sound, as if pretending to be fierce.

"That's right," said her dad softly. "Now, I'm going to clap my hands behind him and see if he reacts." There was a sharp crack as Dr. Adam's palms came together. The puppy didn't move or look around. He sat with his head cocked to one side, looking at Mandy.

"Do you think he's deaf, Dr. Adam?" asked Mr. Taylor.

"I'm afraid it looks that way," Dr. Adam said sadly.

"Oh, no. . . . That's awful! Poor little thing," said Mandy, hugging the little puppy, who looked perfectly happy.

"We thought it was strange that he didn't seem to have learned his name," Mr. Taylor said. "He doesn't come when he's called, either, but we assumed that was because he was so young — and just disobedient."

"I'm sorry," said Dr. Adam, taking another look in Rush's ear. "The exterior part of both ears seems perfectly healthy. There's no blockage. I suspect this is a problem with the nerves inside the ear, in which case it's likely he was born that way. What we need to do is to check up on his littermates, and on his parents, to see if it runs in the family. I think it would be a good idea if you get ahold of Mrs. Merrick and explain the problem."

"Yes, I will. But what can you do for Rush?" asked Mr. Taylor, sounding concerned.

"I'm afraid there's nothing I can do to restore his hearing," Dr. Adam explained sympathetically. "It will be difficult to train him, but he's not going to suffer. He's not in any pain. You'll need to keep him in a secure environment and make sure he's always on a leash when he's out and about. He won't be able to hear the noise of traffic, of course, so you'll need to take extra care on the roads. Do speak to Mrs. Merrick, though," he added. "Information about the other puppies in the litter will be useful. Did you meet the parent dogs when you bought Rush?" Dr. Adam asked.

"Um . . . no," Mr. Taylor said. "No, come to think of it, there didn't seem to be any adult dogs around."

"Hmm." Dr. Adam looked thoughtful. "It's never a good idea to buy a puppy without having seen it with its mother. Bring him back to me for that shot in about three weeks."

"I will," said Mr. Taylor, putting Rush back into the box. "Thanks."

"Good luck," said Dr. Adam.

"Bye, Rush," Mandy said in a small voice. She felt sad to think of the puppy growing up in a world of silence.

When the morning clinic was over, Mandy found her mother relaxing at the kitchen table, drinking a mug of coffee, with the morning papers spread out in front of her.

"Has Dad finished yet, sweetheart?" Dr. Emily asked.

"Yup. It wasn't really a busy morning, was it?" Mandy replied as she pulled out a chair.

"No," her mother agreed. "I wish we had more Saturdays like this."

Mandy sighed and sat down opposite her mother. She picked up part of the newspaper and started flipping through it listlessly.

"You look upset," Dr. Emily said. "Everything all right?"

"An Old English sheepdog puppy came in to see Dad. He found out it was completely deaf," Mandy told her.

Her mom was about to reply when the kitchen door opened.

"Any coffee left in that pot, Emily?" Dr. Adam came into the kitchen taking off his white coat. He flopped into a chair. "I trust Mrs. Ponsonby left Animal Ark in a happier frame of mind," he teased his wife. "I heard all about it from Jean!"

Dr. Emily laughed, and handed him a mug of coffee. "I think I managed to convince her that Toby's smell hadn't caused Pandora to have a fit. Toby's eye needed rinsing out, but he'll survive!"

Mandy was still thinking about Rush. "Dad, will that puppy — Rush — be scared of not being able to hear anything?" she asked suddenly.

"I don't think so," her father replied. "It's likely that he was born deaf. He'll think that silence is normal."

"Mandy was just telling me about this deaf puppy, Adam. Do we know the breeder?" Dr. Emily asked.

"It's one of Mrs. Merrick's pups," her husband told her. "She's said to be a good breeder. But I'm a little concerned. The owner tells me that he didn't see the mother dog with the litter."

"That's odd, if her reputation is anything to go by," Dr. Emily remarked. "She lives over near Walton, doesn't she?"

Dr. Adam nodded. "I think she's a client of Tony Spence's clinic," he said.

"Why do you think that the rest of the litter might be deaf as well, Dad?" Mandy asked, remembering her father's advice to Mr. Taylor to check the dog's brothers and sisters.

"Well, the deafness might be genetic," he replied. "It could have been passed to Rush from his parents. If that's the case, the rest of them might be deaf, too." He sighed.

"Can a puppy get deafness from its parents?" Mandy was puzzled.

"You know how puppies look like their parents?" he asked. "Like when black dogs have black puppies?"

"Yes." Mandy frowned. "It has to do with their genes, doesn't it?"

Mandy's mom nodded. "That's right. A puppy's shape and size — and color — are all passed on from their mother and father."

"And deafness can be passed on, too?" Mandy said.

"Exactly!" Dr. Adam smiled. "That's why good dog breeders choose the parents of their litters very carefully."

"That way," Dr. Emily added, "they can usually stop any problems being passed on to the puppies. So it might be that Rush is just a very unlucky puppy who happens to be deaf. But it's best to check his brothers and sisters, just in case."

"The sad thing about a puppy being born deaf is that it needs extra care for its entire life. The owners don't always realize what they are taking on. Sometimes people find they can't cope with a dog with a problem — and end up abandoning it." Dr. Adam frowned.

Mandy sighed. She hated the thought of an animal being abandoned, just because it was deaf.

"Cheer up," said her mom. "It sounds like that puppy is in safe hands."

Mandy smiled. "I know," she said. "Mr. Taylor wouldn't abandon Rush."

Her dad picked up the paper. "So, what are you doing for the rest of the day?" he asked.

Mandy grinned. "I had a letter in the mailbox this morning." She jumped up and got the brown envelope from the top of the fridge where she'd left it that morning. "It's from the We Love Animals charity."

"Ah!" said Dr. Emily, grinning. "It's that time of year again, is it?"

"It is." Mandy waved the letter at her. "Look." She unfolded the piece of paper and began to read: *"Are you an animal lover? We need you to raise money for animals in danger. Animal lovers from all over the coun-*

*try will be holding a variety of fund-raising events to
support the We Love Animals campaign. If you would
like to be one of them, and if you have a fun, original
idea for an event, then why not fill in the form below
to register your event? The We Love Animals Fund-
raising Day will be on Saturday, June 30."*

"That's pretty soon," Dr. Emily said. "You've only got
a week or two to think of an idea."

"I know," said Mandy. "And I want to come up with
something *really* good again this year!" Mandy gathered
up the letter and leaflets and stood up. "I'll go and call
James."

"Okay," Dr. Adam replied, going back to his paper.
"See you later."

Two

Mandy had arranged to meet James on Meadow Lane. She heard Blackie panting even before she saw him. As they appeared around the corner, the black Labrador was straining on his leash ahead of James.

"Hello, Blackie," Mandy called. Blackie stopped, his ears pricked, then he ran forward, tail wagging, nearly pulling James off his feet as he rushed up to say hello to her. Mandy bent down and ruffled Blackie's silky ears.

"I brought the letter I told you about," she told James, handing him the envelope. "The We Love Animals day is the Saturday after school closes, so we need to decide what to do right away."

James grinned, pushing his hair off his forehead. He looked hot already. "We'll think of something. Come on, I want to let Blackie off his leash before he pulls my arm off!" he said.

"Let's go toward Manor Farm," Mandy suggested, pointing to the path that led back past Animal Ark toward the Greenaways' home.

"You're free!" James told Blackie, bending down to unfasten the leash.

Mandy walked beside James. Blackie raced along ahead of them. He raised his nose and sniffed at the warm summer air. From time to time, he was distracted by the rustling of some small creature in the undergrowth and stopped to tilt his head and listen. Watching him reminded Mandy of Rush.

"Someone brought an Old English sheepdog puppy into the clinic this morning," she told James. "Dad discovered it was deaf."

"Can your dad operate?" James asked, stopping to take a rock out of his sneaker.

"He says he can't do anything — the poor thing was born that way. Dad thinks it might have inherited the deafness from its parents."

James was about to respond, when they noticed a horrible smell. "Ugh!" James exploded indignantly, as Blackie bounded up to them, happily wagging his tail.

The Labrador had gone off to explore under a tree by a bush and had returned triumphant, coated in slimy, smelly manure. The greenish-brown mess oozed over his shoulder blades and dripped down his front legs.

Mandy doubled over with laughter. "Blackie! You stink!" she cried, covering her nose with her hand. "James, do you have any perfume with you?"

"Perfume?" James repeated, wrinkling his freckled nose. "Are you kidding? It's not funny, Mandy! I'll have to give him a bath again. That's the third time this week!" he said angrily.

"Sorry," Mandy muttered sympathetically, trying to suppress her giggles. "It's just that Mrs. Ponsonby brought Toby in with the same problem this morning. She had drenched him in sickening perfume — and got it in his eye. It certainly helped to mask the terrible smell, though."

James laughed. "Blackie! You're a monster," he said heatedly. "Come on, let's go back. Are you going to help wash him?"

"Wash him!" Mandy exclaimed, seizing James's sleeve in her excitement. "That's it!"

"That's what?" James asked, pushing his glasses further up along the bridge of his nose and staring at his best friend. "Have you gone completely out of your mind?"

"We'll wash dogs! We'll charge people for washing their dogs. We'll make tons of money for the We Love Animals fund-raiser!"

"What a great idea!" James breathed, his eyes shining. "I've certainly had enough practice since Blackie decided he was going to roll in every disgusting mess in Welford!"

"Oh, no," Mandy said, looking around. "Blackie's run off again. You'd better put him on the leash and we'll take him back to Animal Ark. I'm sure Mom and Dad will let us use the animal shower."

But Blackie was off again, squeezing through a gap in the bushes that grew along the edge of the path.

"Blackie!" shouted James. The hedge parted. Mandy heard a panting sound as a lolling, dripping, pink tongue appeared in the gap. Then Blackie's shiny, black body squeezed through the hedge and bounded up to James.

"Yuck!" James said in disgust. "Here, let me put this leash on you."

Mandy laughed as James tried to attach the leash to Blackie's collar. "Not much of a walk, was it? Poor Blackie. But we've got lots to do," she told him. "Let's go!"

They walked briskly back to Animal Ark, Blackie trotting along at James's heels. The smell rose around him.

"Let's hope," said James, pinching his nose with his fingers, "that none of the dogs we wash on the day of the fund-raiser has rolled in anything horrible."

"They'd better not," Mandy said. "We won't have a free hand to hold our noses!"

"Maybe we could borrow two of your parents' surgical masks," James suggested, laughing.

As they turned onto the path that would take them back to Animal Ark, Mandy began to run. "Come on, James," she urged. "Hurry up."

James broke into a run, a delighted Blackie following along at his heels. But Mandy was first through the back door into the kitchen, where she almost collided with her mother.

"Yikes! Sorry, Mom. Hi, Dad. Hello, Grandma!" Mandy was gasping for breath as she greeted her grandmother. Mandy's grandparents lived in Lilac Cottage, not far from Animal Ark.

"Is somebody chasing you, Mandy?" laughed her grandmother, who was placing pieces of coffee cake on a large platter.

"Yes, James and Blackie!" Mandy replied, grinning, as James arrived in the kitchen.

"Hmm, something smells good in here," he remarked, closing the door firmly on his foul-smelling dog. Blackie barked in frustration and scraped at the door.

"Oh, he can come in, James," said Dr. Emily. "You know Blackie is always welcome."

"No, he can't," Mandy announced firmly. "Not today. He stinks."

"Not another dog who likes rolling in things?" Dr. Emily inquired, her eyebrows raised.

"Manure," James explained and wrinkled his nose.

"Well, you can put him in the animal shower next door, if you like," Dr. Emily offered, as she set the kitchen table.

"That's what we were hoping," James said. "Thanks, Dr. Emily."

"Mom," Mandy began, collapsing into a chair, "James and I have a great idea. We're going to organize a sponsored dog wash to raise money for the We Love Animals day!" She reached out to take some cake.

"Hands off!" Grandma said sternly, tapping Mandy's fingers with a wooden spoon. "I haven't finished putting them out yet!"

"Would you like a cheese sandwich, James?" Dr. Emily held out a plate and James took one. "That sounds like an excellent idea, Mandy. So where are you going to hold this dog wash?"

"We hadn't thought of that," James admitted, looking at Mandy.

"We'll need a really safe yard," said Mandy, "so the dogs can't escape. We'll also need a hose."

"Blackie hates hoses," James sighed, as the Labrador barked from the other side of the kitchen door.

"Well, you won't be able to do it here at Animal Ark, I'm afraid," Dr. Emily told them. "We're usually busy on Saturday mornings, and we can't have a bunch of overexcited dogs running around upsetting all the patients."

"I suppose you could use our yard," said Grandma thoughtfully, offering Mandy some cake. "But your grandad would have to patch up the holes in the fence first. You can't have dogs escaping into the road! And like Blackie, most dogs aren't too keen on being washed."

"We'll need two people to do the bathing — one to hold, and one to shampoo and rinse," Mandy decided.

James brushed the bread crumbs from around his mouth. "We'll need someone to take care of the dogs while they wait, too. My cousin Jenny's coming to stay at the end of school — she won't mind helping," he said.

"Perhaps your father would give you a hand, too, Mandy," Dr. Emily said, glancing across at her husband. "I can cope with the morning clinic with Simon's help. Maybe Dad can help you to supervise the dogs."

Dr. Adam groaned. "Just what I need — a yard full of unruly wet dogs to look after," he grumbled playfully.

"Dad!" Mandy scolded him. "It's for a good cause!"

"All right, then," Dr. Adam grinned. "You've twisted my arm."

"Thanks, Dad." Mandy smiled. She knew that her dad would enjoy the dog wash almost as much as she would.

"Why don't you make some fliers to put in mail-boxes," Grandma advised, pouring out drinks for everyone. "You'll have to make sure everybody knows about it."

Mandy's eyes were shining. "Yes! Of course! We'll design some posters and put them up all over Welford. That should attract tons of dog owners."

"At last," said James, "a chance to show off my artistic talent."

"What artistic talent?" Mandy teased.

"Oh . . . Mandy, this came for you this morning." Dr. Emily held up a small white envelope. "I mixed it up with my own mail by mistake. Sorry."

"Thanks, Mom," said Mandy, taking the letter from her mother. She studied the postmark. "Oh, look, it must be from John Hardy. It's addressed to both of us, James!" But before they could open it, they heard an indignant scraping at the kitchen door.

"Poor Blackie," said Dr. Emily. "You'd better get back to him. He doesn't sound too happy."

James laughed. "He really is getting fed up. Come on, Mandy. Let's open that letter outside — or Blackie might just break down the door!"

Mandy sat cross-legged on the springy grass and held Blackie at bay with an outstretched arm.

"Sit!" James commanded. Blackie tilted his head at his master and did as he was told. "Good boy," James said. "Hurry up with that letter, Mandy. You're going to have a bath, Blackie. I can't stand the smell much longer." He pinched his nose.

"It's a very short letter," Mandy remarked, scanning the small piece of notepaper. "It just says that he's coming home for the vacation . . . um —" Mandy found the date she was looking for, "— on June fifteenth — he gets out before we do. He'll be back here on the sixteenth."

"Good," James said. "That's great. He'll be here for the fund-raising day."

John Hardy was eleven years old, the same age as James. He was at boarding school in the Lake District, but for vacations he lived with his father, Julian, and his step-mother, Sara, at Welford's Fox and Goose restaurant.

"We'd better write back soon," James decided. "I'm sure he'll want to help with the dog wash."

"Good idea," Mandy agreed. "John will love it — and we're going to need some help." She got to her feet. "It looks like we're going to have a busy afternoon. Let's wash Blackie first, then we can write to John. And then we've got to think about a design for our posters."

"Fine by me," grinned James. "But do you think I'll have time for some of your grandma's coffee cake first?"

Mandy and James were about to take Blackie into the residential block for his shower, when Ted Forrester, the local SPCA inspector, turned up.

"Hi, Ted," Mandy smiled.

"Hello, Mandy, James," he said. He put out a hand to pat Blackie, then quickly withdrew it. "Uh-oh!" He laughed.

"Yes," James said grimly. "It's horrible, isn't it? We're just taking him into Animal Ark for a shower."

"I won't keep you, then. I wanted to see your dad, Mandy. Is he busy? He called a while ago about a pup from Mrs. Merrick's place."

"Hello there, Ted. I thought I heard your voice," Dr. Adam called from the kitchen door. "Thanks for stopping by." He came outside, squinting in the bright afternoon sun.

"No trouble. What's up?" Ted took off his hat.

"I'm not sure," Dr. Adam said, frowning. "We had an Old English sheepdog pup come in this morning. I'm pretty certain it was younger than the owner had been led to believe, and completely deaf. The gentleman said he'd gotten it from Mrs. Merrick. He hadn't seen the puppy with its mother, either. It all seems a little strange."

"You can say that again," Ted replied. "She's supposed to be a good breeder. Of course, it's a hobby for her, rather than a real business. She lives over in Walton, right?"

"Yes, I know her property. Big iron gates shaped like dogs' heads," Dr. Adam said. Then he added, "Of course, this puppy could have been the only one born deaf, but it's strange that the mother dog was missing. I don't want to go poking my nose in where it's not wanted, Ted. You understand."

"Don't worry," Ted reassured him. "I'll do some nosing around. I'll make it a social call, though. I don't want to upset her," he said.

"Thanks, Ted. That will put my mind at ease." Dr. Adam smiled.

"And mine," Mandy said quietly.

"But I have to tell you," Ted Forrester began, "it won't be for a couple of days yet. I'm crazy with work at the moment. I'll get over to her just as soon as I can, all right?" Ted sniffed, then looked around and down at Blackie. "Now, James," he said. "What about that shower for this smelly dog?"

James pushed his glasses higher up on the bridge of his nose and squared his shoulders. "Yes," he said, and turned to Mandy. "Ready for battle?" he asked.

"As ready as I'll ever be!" she laughed. "Let's do it!"

'WE LOVE ANIMALS' CHARITY

Put your money where your heart is

SPONSORED DOG WASH

SATURDAY 31ST JULY
11 A.M.
THE FOX AND GOOSE
WELFORD

Three

Blackie's happily thumping tail drooped suddenly when he spotted the shower. His ears went back. He turned around and tried to slink out of the door, back into the yard.

"Grab him!" James yelled at Mandy, who sprang forward and tucked her fingers firmly through the Labrador's collar.

"Sorry, Blackie," Mandy said as she led him into the cubicle. "You might think you smell wonderful, but we don't!"

"Don't look at me like that, Blackie." James grinned

at the mournful expression on Blackie's face. "You're used to being washed by now."

James put Blackie under the shower head and held him there. Mandy turned on the warm water. Blackie shuddered, then began to shake his fur out. "Ugh!" cried Mandy, as droplets of dirty water flew in all directions. "I'm soaked!"

"We'll have to wear raincoats for the dog wash!" James laughed. When Blackie's coat was completely wet, Mandy turned off the tap. James squeezed a blob of dog shampoo onto Blackie's shoulders and began to massage it into a lather of bubbles. Mandy helped him, working the soap into a froth around Blackie's neck and down his chest. Blackie looked at her accusingly. His nose twitched from the sharp, clean smell of the shampoo.

"There!" James said triumphantly, when every bit of Blackie's thick, black coat was covered. "Now, I'll hold him. Turn on the water again, will you?"

"Right," Mandy said. Blackie shook vigorously as the water cascaded over his shoulders and pooled around his feet. With the palms of his hands, James swept the clean water off the dog's back, leaving his coat standing up in small, wet peaks of fur.

"Now you can let him go," Mandy said. "The door's open."

Blackie wasted no time in making his escape. He ran away, then flung himself onto the warm grass outside and rolled, grunting happily, all four legs waving in the air. Mandy and James sat down on the grass, laughing.

"Just look at him! What a silly dog." James was grinning, while trying to wipe the water off his glasses with his wet T-shirt.

"He smells much better, though," Mandy said.

"Hmm," said James. "But for how long?" He put his glasses back on, then lay back in the sun with his eyes closed.

"Hey!" Mandy poked him in the ribs. "Don't doze off. We've got work to do, remember?" James ignored her, pretending to be asleep. Blackie, in high spirits, trotted over and looked down at his master. He tilted his head, then licked James's cheek with his long, wet tongue.

James sat up. "All right, all right," he grumbled. "I can't fight both of you. Let's take Blackie home now. We can design the posters at my house. That way, we can use the computer."

"Great idea," Mandy said.

Mandy stuck her head through the kitchen door to tell her mom they were going. Then she and James set off on the road in the direction of the Hunters' house.

Passing the Fox and Goose, they spotted Mr. and Mrs. Hardy tidying the window boxes in the front of the low, stone building. Sara Hardy, John's stepmother, looked up.

"Hello, you two," she called. "Blackie's taking you for a walk!" She smiled at the ever-eager Blackie, straining on his leash.

"Hi, Sara," Mandy said. "We've already taken him for one walk today — and had to bathe him afterward! Now he thinks he deserves another."

"Looks like you did a good job," Mr. Hardy observed, stroking Blackie's glossy head. "What a beautiful, shiny coat."

"We've had so much practice washing dogs that we've decided to make some money out of it," James told him. "We're planning a sponsored dog wash to raise money for We Love Animals day."

Sara Hardy smiled, easing off her gardening gloves as she spoke. "That sounds like a good idea." Her cheeks were glowing pink in the warm afternoon sun. "There are certainly plenty of dogs around here, so you'll have lots of customers."

"We're going to ask John to help us," Mandy explained. "We had a letter from him today, saying he'll be back in Welford next week."

"Oh, I'm sure he'd love to get involved!" Julian Hardy sounded pleased. James tugged at Blackie's leash. The Labrador was sticking his nose in the pile of soil and weeds the Hardys had collected below the window boxes. Watching Blackie, Mandy spotted a hose coiled beside the open wooden gate that led into the restaurant's pretty fenced-in yard. It gave her an idea.

"The only problem is, we haven't found anywhere to hold it yet," she told Mr. and Mrs. Hardy. "We'll need a fairly big yard with a wall around it, so that it's safe. There are too many cars at the clinic and . . ." Mandy frowned.

"Here!" Julian Hardy chimed in. "This is the obvious place. Why don't you use the yard of the Fox and Goose?"

"Really?" James said, blinking.

"Are you sure?" Mandy asked, her eyes shining. "That would be great!"

"I think it's a wonderful idea," Sara said, smiling broadly. "After all, it might give us a few extra customers in the restaurant, too."

"Definitely," Mr. Hardy agreed. "When did you want to hold this dog wash, Mandy?"

"The first Saturday of summer vacation," Mandy told him. She nudged Blackie off her foot, where he had just sat down with an impatient little sigh.

"No problem," said Mr. Hardy, putting his arm around his wife. "We'll make that definite then, okay?"

"Thanks a lot, Mr. Hardy!" Mandy was thrilled.

"Yes, thanks, Mr. Hardy. This is going to be fantastic."
James grinned. "Can we tell John that it's going to be
held here at the Fox and Goose when we write to him?"

"Why not?" said Mr. Hardy, stooping to pick up his
gardening tools.

"We should get going," James said, looking at Mandy.
Blackie had begun to tug James off in the direction of
his home.

"Yes. Bye, and thanks again," Mandy called, hurrying after James as Sara Hardy waved.

"That was good luck!" James said, as they rushed along behind an impatient Blackie.

"Yes, it's great," Mandy agreed. "Now, let's get Blackie home and start on those posters."

James and Mandy designed their poster using James's computer. When the printer had delivered a stack of crisp, colored copies, Mandy stood back to admire them.

"What a good team we are," said James, looking proudly at his work.

"It looks great," Mandy agreed. "I can't wait to show Mom and Dad. Will you walk back to Animal Ark with me?"

"It's almost dinnertime," James said doubtfully, looking at his watch.

"I'm sure there'll be tons of food at our house — even enough for you," Mandy teased.

James jumped up. "Great! I'll just tell my dad I'm going. You bring the posters and I'll see you outside."

Mandy was right about there being plenty for dinner. Dr. Emily had just removed a large, sizzling, cheesy pasta dish from the oven when Mandy and James arrived, carrying the pile of posters.

"You've been busy," observed Dr. Adam, who was slicing tomatoes for a salad.

"I hope you've worked up an appetite," Dr. Emily said.

"We have!" Mandy told her, stealing a piece of tomato from her dad's salad bowl. "Can James eat with us?" she asked.

"Yes, of course," smiled Dr. Emily. "You're right on time, too."

"Thanks, Dr. Emily," James grinned. "What do you think of our poster?" He plucked one from the top of the pile and held it up for Mandy's parents to see. Dr. Emily took off her oven mitt. "It's a great picture," she said.

In the middle of the poster, a happy-looking dog was sitting in an old tin bathtub filled with soap bubbles. Dr. Emily began to read aloud: "*Put your money where your heart is.* . . . It's a good slogan, too," she said.

"I think you've done a great job," said Dr. Adam, squeezing Mandy's shoulder gently.

"And we've had some good luck," James told them.

"Oh, yes!" said Mandy. "Mr. and Mrs. Hardy said we can use the Fox and Goose yard for the dog wash!"

"That's nice of them," Dr. Adam remarked.

"Their yard will be ideal for it," said Dr. Emily with a smile.

"I realized it would be perfect when I spotted the hose outside the restaurant — and then I dropped a couple of hints," Mandy confessed.

"Hints!" James scoffed, teasingly. "You were so obvious that even Blackie must have known what you were up to."

"Well, I hope you didn't make nuisances of yourselves," Dr. Emily warned sternly.

"No, we didn't," Mandy protested, making a face at James.

"Well, here's your signed registration form," said her father, handing her an envelope. "You can finish filling it in, now that you know where you're going to hold the dog wash."

"Oh, thanks, Dad." Mandy smiled and put the envelope on the counter.

"Sit down, everyone," said Dr. Emily, who was spooning out mounds of steaming pasta from the pot. "And help yourselves to bread and salad."

"Thanks." James grinned, sitting down.

"We've only printed out about fifteen posters," Mandy told her parents as she piled salad onto her plate. "The printer ran out of paper. Do you think that'll be enough?"

"You could use some copies to put under neighbors' doors," Dr. Adam suggested. "Why don't you go into the clinic and ask Jean to help you photocopy a few more? She's catching up on her filing this evening. I'm sure she won't mind."

"Yes, all right," Mandy said, her mouth full.

"Then we can start putting them up right away," James suggested.

"Maybe we could take one to that dog breeder — Mrs. Merrick is her name, right?" Mandy said. "She must know tons of people with dogs. And we might be able to see her puppies while we're there," she added hopefully.

"Mrs. Merrick's house sounds like the perfect place to start," said her dad. "But finish your dinner first, will you?"

As they cleared the plates away, Dr. Emily looked at her daughter. "Mandy . . ." she began. Mandy looked at her mother. She spoke quietly but her tone was firm. "You'll be careful not to mention this business with that puppy — Rush — while you're there, won't you? Remember, it has nothing to do with us. It's between Mr. Taylor and Mrs. Merrick, okay?"

"I promise." Mandy squeezed her mother's hand. "Don't worry!"

"Okay," said Dr. Emily. "Now, don't stay out late, will you?"

"We won't," promised Mandy, as she headed for the clinic with James.

Jean helped them photocopy a stack of posters and found them some stamps for their envelopes — one letter to John Hardy and the other containing the registration form. Jean offered to mail them on her way home.

"I'll take a bunch of these fliers you've made, too, if you like," she suggested. "I'll drop them off in mailboxes as I go."

Although the clinic photocopier had churned out the posters in black and white, and the golden retriever James had drawn no longer looked quite as handsome sitting in his tin bathtub, they still looked pretty good.

"Very professional," Jean announced as James held one up for her to see. "They're really eye-catching. I like the slogan, too."

Encouraged, Mandy gave her a hug, then headed out the door with James.

They set off down the road to Walton. As they pedaled along side by side, Mandy said, "I hope Mrs. Merrick will let us see her puppies."

"We don't actually know that she has any," James observed.

"I suppose not," said Mandy. "But I'm hoping the

puppy that came into the clinic has some brothers and sisters."

"They might have all been sold by now," James pointed out reasonably.

"Then at least we'll see the mother dog," Mandy said with determination. "I love Old English sheepdogs — they're so big and friendly. Mr. Taylor — that's Rush's owner — told me that they're called sheepdogs because they used to be clipped with the sheep."

"Here," James interrupted, as he slowed his bike to a stop by a corner. "Mrs. Merrick's house is over there," he said, pointing. "Look, those are the gates."

Mandy looked on ahead. She saw two massive wrought-iron gates shaped like the heads of two dogs with pointed noses.

"The gates are really big," James said in a small voice.

"Not the house, though," Mandy whispered. She had jumped off her bike and was looking toward the ordinary-looking bungalow behind the dog's head gates. It sat at the top of a paved driveway. The paint on the walls and around the windows was peeling in places. It looked pretty shabby.

Mandy walked over, unlatched the iron gates, and they went up the driveway to the front door. James took a folded flier out of his pocket and smoothed it over. Then he knocked boldly on the door.

After a few seconds, Mandy heard someone fumbling with the lock inside. Then the door opened, just wide enough for someone to see out. Mandy had a glimpse of a worried-looking face, framed by graying hair.

"Hello!" Mandy said brightly. "Mrs. Merrick? My name is . . ."

"Yes," the woman replied irritably, opening the door a little wider. "Who are you?" She seemed worried.

Mandy tried again. "We're raising money for . . ." she began, speaking clearly and rather loudly, trying to be firm.

"Oh, no. . . . Not now," the woman pleaded. "I'm so sorry, but I can't give you anything. Some other time, perhaps. Good-bye."

Mrs. Merrick disappeared, slamming the door in their faces. James looked at Mandy, speechless.

"Well!" Mandy said indignantly. "What do you think of that?"

Four

The days leading up to the end of the school year were very busy and seemed to go by in a blur as Mandy and James planned for the dog wash. They decided to spread the word about the fund-raising event as far and wide as possible. They put up posters in the waiting room at Animal Ark, on the school notice board, in Welford's post office, and on the church porch.

When John Hardy had arrived home from school, Mandy and James went to see him at the Fox and Goose. He was as excited about the dog wash as they were.

"Dad's going to move things around in here on the

day," he told Mandy and James, leading them outside to the large fenced-in backyard. "He's making space for us to wash the dogs near the hose here. We're going to put out extra chairs for the dog owners and there will be umbrellas for shade if it's hot."

"Let's hope so," said James. "We're going to get pretty wet."

"It doesn't matter," Mandy told them. "It's going to be a lot of fun. Let's just hope tons of people turn out."

"I saw your poster, James," John said. "It looks really good." James's face flushed pink with embarrassment.

"Thanks," he mumbled.

"Everything's going according to plan," Mandy said happily. "All we have to hope for now is that it doesn't rain on Saturday!"

The Saturday of the dog wash dawned bright and sunny. When Mandy looked out of the bedroom window, there wasn't a cloud in the sky and she heaved a sigh of relief. A rainy day would have spoiled everything.

Mandy was just clearing away the breakfast dishes when there was a knock at the kitchen door. Dr. Emily answered the door. It was James, along with Blackie, who ran into the kitchen. The Labrador seized one of Dr. Adam's tennis shoes and paraded around with it in his mouth.

"He's really excited," James apologized, puffing, as he grabbed at the shoe.

"*He's* excited!" Dr. Emily laughed, glancing at Mandy. "Then it must be infectious."

James was wearing a pair of shorts and a T-shirt. He held up a plastic bag to show Mandy. "I brought a change of clothes — in case we get soaked," he told her.

"Good idea!" she laughed. "Well, we'd better go. We've got to be ready to start by eleven, and it's ten o'clock now. We'll need time to set things up."

"I'm ready," James told her. "Jenny arrived last night. She's going to meet us there."

Mandy picked up a bag filled with plastic bottles of dog shampoo. "Will you make sure Dad comes over in time, Mom?" she asked.

Dr. Emily nodded. "He's got a few things to do in the clinic — but he'll be there. I hope it all goes smoothly. I'll come as soon as the clinic is finished," she promised. "Have fun!"

"We will. Thanks," called Mandy, as the kitchen door slammed loudly behind her.

The Fox and Goose's backyard had been transformed. Mr. Hardy had moved the wooden tables, benches, and assorted chairs to the far end, leaving plenty of room for a crowd of excited dogs and their owners.

Mandy beamed, looking around at the yard. "Oh, this is great. Thank you!"

"Well, it's for a good cause," Sara Hardy smiled, surveying the pile of equipment that James had just dumped on the grass.

"Sara," John asked, "can we use that big table in the kitchen to put out here? Don't you think we'll need a table, Mandy?"

"Yes. Someone will have to stand behind it and take the money as people come in," Mandy agreed. "Maybe Dad can do that. James has gotten a big glass jar from his mom to put the money in."

"Good idea," John said, in his best businesslike manner. "I'll go and get the table. Will you help me, James?"

"Okay," said James. "Can I leave Blackie loose out here, Mrs. Hardy?"

"Yes, he'll be fine in the yard. He can't get out." Sara Hardy smiled.

"Here's Jenny!" Mandy called, rushing over to meet James's cousin at the gate. They had met when Mandy had gone with James to spend a week's vacation in the Welsh fishing village where Jenny lived.

"Hello, Mandy," Jenny said, a bit shyly, in her soft

Welsh accent. She wore her dark hair in a ponytail, just as Mandy remembered her.

"Hi, Jenny!" Mandy smiled. "Thanks for coming. It's great to see you. I'm really glad we've got you to help. Would you mind hanging this sign on the gate for me? It's almost eleven — time for people to start arriving."

"Important! Please keep the gate closed," Jenny read. "Okay." She grinned and hurried off to the gate.

"Mandy!" James said urgently. "Look! There are people here already." Mandy looked. A couple she didn't know had come hesitantly through the gate and into the yard. They had a big, hairy dog on a leash.

"Are you open yet?" the woman inquired. "We were passing and saw your poster."

"Certainly!" grinned Mandy. "Bring him in. What's his name?"

"Mucky," said the woman, ruffling the dog's coat affectionately. "And it suits him! He's in need of a bath, I'm afraid."

James had taken off his shoes in preparation for a good soaking. "How does Mucky feel about being washed?" he asked cautiously, taking the dog's leash.

"Oh, he loves a bath, don't you, Mucky?" grinned the man.

Mandy was relieved. At least their first customer

wouldn't be a tricky one. She spotted her father chatting to Julian Hardy and waved to him. "Dad! We've got our first customer!"

"Great!" said Dr. Adam, smiling. "Well, get started and send them over my way to pay when you're finished, okay?"

In no time at all, the yard was filled with chatting people and excited dogs. Mandy could hardly believe how many people had seen their posters. Welford's dog owners had turned out in full force to support them, and there were quite a few strangers among the crowd, too.

Mr. Markham, the chairman of the church council, brought his beagle, Bunty, to be washed, and there was a difficult moment when the beagle tried to frighten Ms. Martin's Yorkshire terrier, Snap. Betty Hilder brought a young rescued dog from her animal sanctuary, and even Mrs. Ponsonby came, with Pandora tucked under her arm and Toby straining on a leash.

Mandy, James, Jenny, and John got to work and they soon had an efficient production line going. Pet owners were strolling around with cold drinks in their hands, as they waited for their dog's turn.

"Sara says my dad's going to give a donation to the fund because of the extra money he made in the restau-

rant," John reported, as he joined Mandy, who was rinsing off a corgi named Jack.

"Oh, that's great!" Mandy said gratefully. The dog
wash was going to be a huge success.

"Look who's next," hissed James, above the sound of
yapping. Mandy glanced up to see Ernie Bell holding
Pandora the Pekingese. Mrs. Ponsonby hovered nearby,
looking worried. She wore a wide-brimmed straw hat
decorated with silk flowers.

"I don't believe it," Mandy gasped. "Mrs. Ponsonby is
going to let us wash Pandora," she whispered.

"Really, Mr. Bell," Mrs. Ponsonby was protesting. "I
don't think Pandora will appreciate the hose one bit.
She prefers a bath of warm . . ."

"Now, Mrs. Ponsonby," soothed Ernie, interrupting
her. He stroked Pandora's head and she panted even
harder. "I bet she'll love a cool shower on a hot day like
this. You just leave her to me. We'll soon have her looking as elegant as you are. And may I say that's a very
handsome hat you're wearing today, Mrs. P?"

"Oh, thank you," trilled Mrs. Ponsonby, smiling broadly.
Then her smile faded and she looked very serious.
"Now, you will take care with my Pandora, won't you?"

Mandy laughed and whispered to the others, "Ernie's
been flattering Mrs. Ponsonby. That's how he's persuaded her to let us wash Pandora!" She let go of the

corgi's collar and the little dog tore off to find a patch of green grass to roll on.

"You're doing a great job." Mandy heard Dr. Emily's voice and looked up to see her mother smiling down at them.

"Oh, Mom!" said Mandy. "You're here! It seems to be going really well."

"Let me give you a tip." Dr. Emily spoke softly. "Use just a sponge on Pandora. You don't want to get shampoo in her eyes."

"No, we don't," James said, grimacing.

Mandy could just imagine the scene with Mrs. Ponsonby if anything happened to Pandora.

The Pekingese submitted meekly to the wet sponge, while Ernie Bell offered advice from a nearby bench. "Go ahead and get her wet!" he urged Mandy. "Give her a real bath. She's a dog, not a doll!"

"Ernest Bell!" scolded Mrs. Ponsonby, trying to keep Toby from joining in Pandora's bath. "Pandora doesn't *like* water, I tell you. Don't interfere!"

Two hours later, Mandy had lost count of the number of dogs they had washed. She was hot and tired but she was enjoying herself so much she didn't care. As she looked around the yard she noticed that there were only a few dogs still waiting for their turn.

"Phew!" gasped James, sitting back on the grass. "It feels like we've washed every dog in Yorkshire!"

"I think we might have," said John, passing around the tray of cold drinks that Sara had given him. Mandy took one of the plastic cups and drank gratefully.

"My fingers are numb," Jenny announced.

"Hmm. Mine, too," Mandy said, examining them as she crunched on a piece of ice.

"Just one more to go, everyone," said Mr. Hardy. "I think that's it, after this next little fellow. Every dog in Welford must be squeaky clean — good work."

The last dog to be washed was a small, nervous cocker spaniel. He shook his head vigorously, sending suds of shampoo flying off his long, curly-haired ears. Mandy and James rinsed him off as quickly as possible and gave him back to his owner, who was hovering nearby, holding a towel she had brought with her.

At last, it was over. Mandy sat down in the wet and soapy grass, exhausted. "That was fun," she said, grinning at her friends. "But I'm glad we're finished."

"Me, too," James sighed. "I'm soaked!"

"At least it's a hot day," Jenny said. "I wouldn't have liked getting this wet otherwise."

"What a team!" John said, patting James on the back. "We could go into business."

"No, thank you," James said firmly. "I feel as if I'll never get rid of the smell of dog shampoo!"

Mandy stood up slowly and stretched. She went to take the notice off the gate. Water from the hose had run down the gently sloping lawn and collected at the wooden gate. The tap had been turned off but it was still trickling under the bottom of the gate and into the parking lot beyond.

"Oops," Mandy muttered to herself. "I think we've probably flooded Mr. Hardy's parking lot." She unlatched the gate and looked out. The water had streamed out and formed an impressive puddle. As Mandy looked around, she gasped.

A puppy was sitting in a shallow puddle just to the right of her bare feet. Mandy looked down at its little face, and the tangled, shaggy coat. She took the little dog gently in her arms. Its feet scrambled with fear as Mandy picked it up. Then, feeling the warmth of her arms, it began to relax against her. The puppy snuggled closer, shivering, and gave a tiny whimper.

"Oh!" Mandy said softly. "Oh, you poor little thing. What are you doing here? You're only a few weeks old! Where did you come from?"

The puppy looked a little bit like Rush, but Mandy could feel the bones through this pup's skin and she remembered how plump, cuddly, and well-fed little Rush was. This puppy had been neglected. Its fur was matted and its belly was swollen beneath the skinny rib cage — a sign of worms, Mandy remembered.

Mandy felt a hot flash of anger surge through her. "Who," she asked the little dog, "would let you get into this state?" She glanced around, peering into the few remaining parked cars, searching for the puppy's owner. There was no one around.

Moving very gently, Mandy carried the little puppy through the gate into the yard. "James!" she called. "Come quickly!"

Five

James and the others were cleaning up. Mandy saw him turn around when he heard the urgency in her voice. He hurried over to where she was standing just inside the gate, cradling the shivering puppy protectively.

"What on earth have you got there?" James called, as he came toward her.

"It's an Old English sheepdog puppy," Mandy said. "I found it sitting in a puddle outside the gate."

"All alone? In the parking lot?" James asked. "Any sign of the owner?" He put out a finger and stroked the pup's head lightly. The puppy shrank back and buried its nose in Mandy's forearm.

"No, everyone's gone. Let's go and find my mom and dad," Mandy said.

"They're over there, in the yard with Mr. Hardy," James told her.

Dr. Adam looked up and called out to Mandy as she approached. "You've done really well — you've collected a lot of money!" he told her.

"Forget about that, Dad," Mandy cried. "Look what I found!"

Dr. Emily, Sara and Julian Hardy, and John and Jenny, who had been picking up cups from the yard, gathered around her. The puppy, alarmed at all the strange faces, squirmed uncomfortably, then edged its way upward and snuggled under Mandy's chin.

"A lost puppy?" Dr. Emily frowned in concern. "It looks as if it needs a bath, doesn't it?"

"It's lost — or been abandoned," Mandy said unhappily. "There's no one around who it could belong to and it doesn't have a name tag. And look at it, Mom, it looks just awful!"

Blackie raised his nose and tried to sniff at the interesting bundle, as Dr. Emily lifted the puppy gently from Mandy's arms. "It's about twelve or thirteen weeks old, I would guess," said Mandy's mom. She ran her fingers lightly around the puppy's frail body and looked at the rims of its blue eyes. "Poor thing! I guess you've been wandering around for a while — you're very thin." Dr. Emily paused and lifted the puppy to look at its swollen stomach. "It's a girl," she told them.

"Oh, she's so sweet," Jenny said.

"Should I go and have a look around outside — to see if I can spot anyone who might know something about her?" John asked.

"I've looked," said Mandy, "and I'm sure there's no one around."

Dr. Adam took the puppy from his wife, checking its coat for signs of fleas. Mandy stood beside him and James, while Jenny and John hovered nearby, looking worried.

"She might be in need of some liquid if she's a stray. I think we'd better get her to the clinic and have a good look at her," Dr. Adam said at last.

"Can I come with you?" James asked.

"I'll go with John," Jenny said. "We'll see if we can find anyone in town who knows where she came from."

"I've got just the name for you," said Mandy, looking at the little pup. "We'll call you Puddles."

Dr. Emily raised her eyebrows. "Mandy, you know the rules . . ."

Mandy knew she was not supposed to give stray animals names, but she was determined that the defenseless, abandoned puppy should be cared for now. "She should have a name — that's the least she deserves," she protested.

"You go on back to Animal Ark," Sara Hardy said, putting a hand on Mandy's shoulder. "Julian and I will finish cleaning up here. And if anyone comes looking for a puppy, we'll send them straight over to you."

Back at the clinic, the puppy seemed more nervous than ever. She wiggled in Mandy's arms, trying to hide by burying her head. Mandy spoke soothingly to her, and Puddles responded gratefully by licking Mandy's chin.

Dr. Adam examined her carefully. "She needs a good bath, Mandy," he said. "She's had stomach trouble and she's dehydrated and weak. I'll give her worming medicine and put her on an IV to get some fluid into her."

"Can't I feed her, Dad?" Mandy pleaded. "She's so thin — she must be starving."

"Not just yet, sweetheart. We'll try her on a small amount of food a little later. Let's see how she responds to the fluid first."

Mandy stood with James, watching the puppy hunched miserably on the examination table. Puddles hung her head, refusing to look at them. "How can people be so cruel?" James asked angrily.

"It never ceases to amaze me, James," Dr. Adam sighed, "but they can — and they are."

"This is the second Old English sheepdog puppy with some kind of problem," Mandy said.

"You're right, Mandy," confirmed Dr. Emily, glancing at her husband. "This puppy would be about the same age as the deaf puppy that came in to see you — Rush, wasn't it?"

"That's right," said Dr. Adam, looking into Puddles's

ear. "Mr. Taylor brought Rush in about . . . let's see . . . three weeks ago now. It might be a coincidence, but this pup could easily be a sister to little Rush. Luckily, this puppy has perfectly good hearing."

"It's that Mrs. Merrick again!" Mandy declared furiously. "That woman . . ."

"Hold on, Mandy." Dr. Emily held up her hand. "We have no idea whether this poor puppy has anything to do with Mrs. Merrick. You can't go around blaming people when we don't have the facts."

"Well," Mandy began. "She breeds Old English sheepdogs, doesn't she?"

"That's no evidence at all," Dr. Adam pointed out gently. "This puppy may have been abandoned from a car by her owners as they passed through Welford. Or she may have escaped from home. Someone might be frantically looking for her."

"It's strange that she turned up at the Fox and Goose just as we were having the dog wash," James mused.

"Mom, do you think somebody put her out of their car at the restaurant because they knew there would be dog lovers there?" Mandy asked.

Dr. Emily put an arm around Mandy. "I don't know, honey. The main thing is, she's safe with us here now. We'll take care of her."

There was a soft knocking on the door of the exam room and Mandy's heart leaped. Was this Puddles's owner coming to look for her?

"Only me . . ." Ted Forrester stuck his head through the door.

"Hello, Ted!" said Dr. Adam and Dr. Emily together.

"I stopped in at the Fox and Goose and Mrs. Hardy told me about the puppy Mandy found," Ted told them. "Anything I can do?"

"We were just discussing how it might have gotten there, Ted," Dr. Adam said.

"And speculating on whether it might be one of Mrs. Merrick's pups . . ." Dr. Emily added.

Ted walked over to the examination table and stooped to look at Puddles. "Hello there, little one," he began, tipping the little dog's chin up with his finger.

"If it *is* one of Mrs. Merrick's litter," said Mandy heatedly, as Ted crooned and stroked Puddles, "then she should be ashamed of herself! First breeding a deaf puppy and now . . ."

"Now, Mandy," Ted said, straightening up and looking at her. "I know she breeds this type of dog, but we don't *know* it's one of hers, do we?"

"I suppose not . . ." Mandy mumbled. She knew she

was being unreasonable but she couldn't help herself. She felt sure that Puddles had something to do with the Merrick kennels.

"Mrs. Merrick might have sold this puppy in good faith to someone who decided simply to get rid of it, you know," Ted continued.

"Have you spoken to Mrs. Merrick about Rush, Ted?" Dr. Adam asked.

"I can't say that I have," admitted Ted. "It's been a hectic time for me lately — but I will, I promise." He glanced at Mandy. "But we can't go upsetting her by going around making wild accusations."

"It's a strange coincidence," Mandy insisted.

"Well, never mind about that. Let's get on with getting this puppy well, shall we?" Dr. Emily said briskly, changing the subject. She steered Mandy toward the sink. "You run some warm water in there, and I'll get some shampoo. We'll clean her up before we do anything else. Okay?"

"How's her health?" Ted asked Dr. Adam.

"She's very dehydrated. I would guess she's been wandering for a few days. Being so young, she's lucky to be alive," Dr. Adam replied.

"Well, I'll let my colleagues know. They'll put the word out and maybe an owner will come forward. And

I'll also notify the police. Anyone who's lost a pet is likely to report it to them." Ted smiled and turned to Mandy and James.

"Thanks, Ted," Dr. Adam said. "I suppose I'd better be getting back to the Fox and Goose. I've left the money we collected with Julian Hardy."

"I'll let you go, then." Ted waved from the door. "Good luck with the pup. Bye, all."

Mandy had half filled the big stainless steel sink with warm water. Puddles's tiny feet scrambled frantically as she was lowered into it. Mandy felt sorry for the frightened puppy. "It has to be done," Dr. Emily said firmly. "She'll be a lot happier when we've cleaned up the mess she's made of herself."

"James? Mandy?" Jenny was calling from the waiting room. "Are you here?"

"I'll go," said James.

"Bring her in here, if you like," Dr. Emily said.

James was back a moment later, with Jenny and John. They gathered around the sink, looking at the wet little puppy.

"Did you find anyone who knows Puddles?" James asked eagerly.

"Nobody," Jenny said. "We asked around — we even

knocked on a few doors — but nobody knows anything about her."

"Most people we asked said to come here — to Animal Ark — for help," John said.

Dr. Emily washed Puddles as gently as she could. The water turned a murky gray-brown from the dirt in the puppy's coat. With a wad of cotton balls, Mandy wiped away the encrusted muck around Puddles's blue eyes. She gazed up at Mandy trustingly.

"What are you going to do?" Jenny asked.

"The SPCA knows about her, and they'll let the police know," Mandy said. "We'll keep her here with us until she's stronger."

"Let's hope someone will claim her soon," Dr. Emily said with a smile, reaching into a nearby cabinet for a towel.

On the exam table, Mandy patted and gently rubbed Puddles until the towel had soaked up almost all the water from her coat.

"She looks like a different dog!" John exclaimed.

It was true. The puppy's dirty, matted fur was now a snowy white. Dr. Emily began to comb out some of the twisted knots of hair, using her fingers to pry them apart.

"She's so tired," Mandy said, as Puddles rolled over on the towel and began to lick listlessly at one wet paw.

"She needs a good sleep," Dr. Emily said. Puddles was quickly drying off and her puppy fur had begun to fluff out. It was streaked with very dark gray, almost black, and one of her feet was darker still.

"She's so tiny," Jenny sighed. "I love her one black sock."

Dr. Emily gently slipped a syringe into Puddles's front leg. She hardly noticed the needle going in. Dr. Emily taped a tiny tube into place, to carry saline solution into Puddles's body. The little puppy looked at her leg curiously, and tried to nibble at the tape.

"Come along, young lady," said Mandy's mom, lifting the sleepy puppy into her arms. Mandy picked up the plastic bottle that held the saline and followed her mother around the table and toward the door.

"I can see you've done this before," Jenny said quietly, looking impressed. Mandy grinned, and nodded.

"I get plenty of practice here," she said.

In Animal Ark's residential unit, Mandy and her mom put Puddles into a small kennel lined with a fleece rug. Dr. Emily hung the bag of saline on a hook outside the kennel and carefully closed the door. "We must let her sleep. I'll check on her in a few hours' time," Dr. Emily said. "Now, what about something to drink and a bite to eat for everyone?"

Mandy didn't feel very hungry. She wanted to stay

and comfort the puppy. But Puddles's head had drooped onto her front paws and, as Mandy watched, she sighed deeply as her eyes closed.

"Okay," she said, smiling at her mom. "That sounds like a good idea."

Six

The next morning, Mandy ran downstairs and straight out to the residential unit to check on their new patient.

"She's had a good, long sleep," said Dr. Adam. "I've taken her off the drip and my guess is she's ready for something to eat." Mandy gazed in at the little pup. Puddles blinked her blue eyes and looked slowly around her kennel, as if trying to remember where she was. Then she shuffled forward and put her wide, black button nose up against the wire mesh, trying to sniff at Mandy.

"Can I take her out?" Mandy pleaded.

"I bet she'd like some attention." Dr. Adam grinned.

He unlatched the kennel and stood aside. "There you are . . . I'll go and find her some breakfast!"

Puddles sneezed violently as Mandy put her hands gently around her pink tummy. "Oops! Bless you!" Mandy said, and lifted Puddles into her arms. The puppy's long fur was as soft as silk. She sniffed at Mandy's chin, then found her finger and began to chew on it with needle-sharp teeth. "Ouch!" Mandy pulled back her finger. "Here, look what Dad's got for you."

Dr. Adam had spooned some canned chicken and rice into a bowl. It was a special mix for animals that had been ill. He held it under the puppy's nose. She whimpered and began to squirm in Mandy's arms to get free.

"All right." Mandy laughed, putting her down. "Now, don't gobble it all at once or you might choke."

Puddles ate daintily but hungrily, then licked the bowl clean with a small pink tongue. Then she sat down and licked her lips. Mandy laughed.

"How's she doing?" asked Dr. Emily, appearing at the door of the residential unit.

"She's much better this morning, Mom," Mandy told her happily. "She's eaten and she seems more cheerful." She looked at Puddles, who was taking small, hesitant steps around the floor. "Can she go outside on the grass? She might want to . . . oh! Too late!"

"I'll clean it up!" Dr. Emily said.

"I'd offer to help but I haven't had *my* breakfast yet!" Dr. Adam grinned. He turned to Mandy. "The puppy should stay indoors a bit longer, Mandy. I want to be sure that she's free of infection. Oh, and by the way, I've written out a check for the money you collected yesterday, so you can mail it later."

"Thanks, Dad," Mandy said. "I want to make sure the money gets to the We Love Animals fund as soon as possible." She waved to Puddles who was having her gums examined by Dr. Emily. "I'll come and see you later," she told the puppy.

Dr. Adam yawned. "I'm starving. It's way past my breakfast time. Anyone for scrambled eggs?"

Mandy had just finished washing the last of the breakfast dishes when there was a knock on the kitchen door. It was James.

"Hi, Mandy." He smiled as he flicked his hair off his forehead. "I came to see how that puppy is doing."

"Come in," Mandy said, moving aside to let him in. "We checked on her this morning and she seems a bit better. But Dad says she has to stay in the kennel for a while." She sat down on a kitchen chair opposite her friend. "James, I've been thinking . . ." Mandy folded her arms.

"What about?" James looked at her warily. He took off his glasses and polished them on his sleeve.

"We ought to go back to Mrs. Merrick's house," Mandy said. "I'm sure these poor puppies have something to do with her. We should see if we can find out anything."

"What do you mean?" James asked, putting his glasses back on.

"I want to take a look around." Mandy sounded serious. "Someone's got to do *something*."

"We'd have to be careful. Remember what Ted Forrester said . . ." James began.

"It'll be okay," Mandy said firmly. "We can pretend to be interested in buying a puppy and just ask some questions."

James was doubtful. "She didn't want to talk to us last time."

"But she thought we were collecting money. If we say we want to buy a puppy, she'll have to let us in, won't she?" Mandy reasoned.

"I suppose so," James said, looking worried. Then he brightened. "I bet we could tell her about finding Puddles, and see what her reaction is."

"That's a good idea." Mandy threw the damp hand towel onto the rack. "We'll go this morning."

"Okay," James agreed. "I'll go home and get my bike."

"Will Jenny want to come with us?" Mandy asked.

James shook his head. "She's waiting for a phone call from her parents. They're traveling in Finland on business, and they promised to call her this morning," James explained, following Mandy out into the yard where Dr. Emily was watering the roses.

"Hello, James." She smiled, looking up from her work.

"Hi, Dr. Emily," James replied.

"Mom," Mandy began, "we're going for a bike ride."

"That sounds like a good idea. It's a nice day," Dr. Emily said, looking up at the deep blue sky.

"We thought we'd go back over to Mrs. Merrick's house and ask if we can see her puppies," Mandy said casually.

"Well, I suppose there's no harm in asking to see them." Dr. Emily went back to her watering. "But, remember, she may not want you there. Just be careful and don't make a nuisance of yourself, will you?"

"We won't. Promise!" Mandy said. She turned eagerly to James. "Meet you outside the post office in ten minutes."

"Okay." James waved as he headed off down the driveway.

*   *   *

Mandy's heart was hammering slightly as she knocked on Mrs. Merrick's front door.

"Yes? Can I help you?" A girl of about seventeen stood in the doorway. She had a pale, oval face and thick chestnut-colored hair that hung to her shoulders. Her fingers were looped through the collar of a large adult sheepdog.

"Yes, please," Mandy smiled. "Um . . . we would like to see the puppies."

"My mother isn't here," the girl told them. "She had to go out. I'm Tracy. Are you interested in buying a puppy?" She frowned and looked past Mandy and James as if expecting to see their parents in the driveway.

"We know that your mother breeds Old English sheepdogs," Mandy explained. "We'd love to see them . . ."

"If you've got any pups at the moment," James added, nudging Mandy with his elbow. Tracy suddenly smiled. She rubbed her eyes and pushed the hair back off her face with her hands. She let go of the dog, who took a step forward and peered docilely up at Mandy and James through a thick fringe of white fur. Mandy stroked his head. She couldn't see its eyes at all.

"Got any? We've got twelve at the moment," Tracy told them. "I'm exhausted looking after them all. You

wouldn't believe what hard work they are." Tracy stepped aside. "Why don't you come in and take a look?"

"Oh, thank you so much!" Mandy said, relieved. They followed Tracy through the dim interior of the house, into a big kitchen with a tiled floor. A barricade of heavy crates had been used to confine the pups in a small area. Mandy could hear faint whimpering and scuffling sounds, and a few louder, more determined howls.

"Over here," Tracy was saying, sliding the heavy boxes to one side. The puppies, seeing the strangers, shrank back, then scampered away to take refuge on a heap of old cushions in a large cardboard box. The box had a large U-shape cutout on one side, so the puppies could hop in and out.

"Oh, look!" Mandy said, delighted with the shaggy pups. "Aren't they gorgeous?"

Tracy said nothing. She folded her arms across her chest.

"They're great!" James exclaimed, looking at the tangle of pale furry bodies and shiny black noses. The puppies peeked out from behind one another and blinked at Mandy and James, but seemed reluctant to come near the strangers.

"Can we touch them?" Mandy asked Tracy.

She nodded and yawned. "Of course. I'm going to

make myself a sandwich. I haven't had any breakfast yet and I'm starving. So if you wouldn't mind keeping an eye on them for me, that would be great," she said. "Don't let any escape, for heaven's sake!" She yawned again.

Mandy noticed shadows under Tracy's eyes. "Oh, don't worry. We'll take care of them. You have a break." Mandy smiled.

A telephone rang in the hallway, and Tracy sprinted away to answer it. The adult dog lay down on the kitchen floor and Mandy and James stepped over into the puppies' enclosure, pulling the barricade shut behind them. One of the larger pups gave a fierce little growl and took a step forward, sniffing at Mandy's outstretched fingers.

"Hello," Mandy said softly, crouching down to greet the little dog. "Come and say hello . . ." Mandy expected the puppy to jump up at her. She loved the comical curiosity of puppies, and the way they responded trustingly to anyone who was kind to them. But this pup was different. He and the other pups seemed reluctant to come near. The puppy turned around and went back into the box over the heads of a few smaller, sleeping puppies.

"James!" Mandy whispered. "They're behaving sort of strangely, aren't they?"

"What do you mean?" James whispered back. He was kneeling on the newspapers and had just noticed a dark wet patch spreading across the fabric of his jeans. He wrinkled his nose.

"Well, they don't seem playful or interested ..." Mandy couldn't quite explain what was wrong.

"Probably sleepy," James said. "Shh, that girl's coming back."

Tracy came into the kitchen, her sandals making little tapping sounds on the tiles. She buttered a slice of bread and then hunted around in the fridge for something.

Mandy stood up. "The pups are all so sweet," she said to Tracy. "How on earth do people choose?"

"Do you want a male or female? That's a start," Tracy said without turning around. She was slicing cheese from a big yellow block. Mandy looked at James, who shrugged at her. "Um ... a girl, probably," Mandy said quickly.

James had started creeping across the expanse of newspaper with his fingers stretched out, trying to coax a tiny puppy forward. It whimpered, then yawned and toppled over. The adult dog wandered over to the barricade and put its large, square muzzle over the top to look in.

"What an enormous litter!" Mandy said, wondering

why the puppies varied in size as much as they did. Tracy glanced over her shoulder. "We've got a mixed bunch here — about four separate litters," she said, through a mouthful of cheese sandwich. "Maybe more — I've lost count."

"What?" Mandy asked. "Really? How come?" She stood up, frowning.

"Well, my mother does run a business here, you know," Tracy said sharply. Mandy decided it was best not to ask any more questions. Tracy yawned again and rubbed her eyes. "Here, Troy. Here, boy!" Tracy called the adult dog to her side.

"Can we help you with the puppies, Tracy?" Mandy asked hopefully. "I mean, James and I love dogs. We'd love to spend some time helping to feed them, or clean up, or something . . . anything."

"Yes, we really would," James confirmed. He had pulled a puppy into his lap and was fiddling with its tiny ears.

"Really?" Tracy had brightened. She came over, her sandwich in her hand. "I could really use some help. They need their area cleaned, as you can probably smell. And feeding them all is a nightmare — some of the little ones are still on bottles." Then she hesitated. "I can't pay you, you know."

"Oh, we don't want any money!" Mandy told her.

Then, she asked the question she had been trying to hold back. "Where is . . . where *are* . . . the mother dogs?"

"Look, I told you," Tracy said, "we're running a business here. I've had to give up college to help my mother, you know, and . . ."

To Mandy's horror, she saw that Tracy's eyes were wet with tears.

"All right," said James, getting quickly to his feet. "Where do you keep the bucket and mop?" he asked. "Let's start."

"Oh, look, I'm sorry," Tracy said miserably. "It's just that I'm tired, really. I didn't mean to snap at you."

"That's all right." Mandy smiled. "We'd like to help. What can we do?"

"You know, we found an Old English sheepdog puppy just like these," James said suddenly. "It was wandering outside the Fox and Goose in Welford."

Tracy, who was delving into a tall closet in search of a bucket, spun around and stared at James. "Really?" she asked, her eyes wide.

"Yes," Mandy said in what she hoped was a casual voice. "It's very young and it was in a terrible state. My mom and dad are vets, and they've been looking after it in the residential unit at Animal Ark."

"What did it look like?" Tracy asked anxiously.

James looked at Mandy. "It's about twelve or thirteen weeks, we think," Mandy told her. "But it was very thin and sad-looking — and its coat was a mess," Mandy finished.

"One very dark gray foot — the other three white?" Tracy asked, her voice hopeful.

"Yes, that's it. Exactly," Mandy confirmed.

"Petal!" Tracy breathed, covering her face with her hands. "Petal! I can't believe it! You *found* her! Is she safe? Is she all right?"

"She *is* one of your puppies!" Mandy cried. "She's fine, Tracy," she added reassuringly. "Don't worry. She's dehydrated because she had an upset stomach, so she's a little weak but . . ." Mandy stopped. Tracy's thin shoulders were heaving. From behind the hands that covered her face Mandy and James could hear muffled sobs.

Seven

Tracy Merrick was crying noisily. Mandy looked at James in alarm, and he shrugged his shoulders. She stepped across the barricade of crates and hurried to Tracy's side. "Don't cry, Tracy," she pleaded. "Puddles — Petal — is safe. What happened to her?"

Tracy sniffed loudly. "Mom was furious," she mumbled through her tears. "It was a few days ago, now. I must have left the barricade open and Petal squeezed through. She was the liveliest of the litter. She was always trying to escape and explore. She got out of the kitchen door and I didn't notice. Then, when I went to open the front door . . ."

James put the sheepdog puppy he'd been playing with back on the cushion and joined Mandy and Tracy. Troy, the adult dog, was staring mournfully up at Tracy.

"Well, it's good news that she's safe, isn't it?" Mandy asked, wishing Tracy would stop crying. Her nose was very red and her skin was blotchy.

"I suppose so," Tracy said, sniffing. "It's just that — well, we've got too many puppies and when Mom has to go out . . . I thought . . ." She paused and gasped, covering her face again. "I thought that Petal was dead! She was my favorite, too."

"It's okay, Tracy," Mandy said soothingly. "We found her and she's doing fine. You could come and visit her at Animal Ark." Mandy didn't want Tracy to take Puddles back. Mrs. Merrick would only sell the puppy. Tracy had said herself that the puppies were only a business.

Tracy snatched a tissue from a box on a small kitchen table, then sat down with a heavy sigh. She blew her nose loudly, making Troy prick up his ears.

"Yes," she said wearily. "I'd like to come and see Petal — as soon as I can get away. Now . . ." Suddenly, Tracy sat up straight and businesslike. "I need to get to work. Mom will be so relieved if everything's done when she gets home."

"Has she been away for long?" Mandy asked, eyeing

the pile of unwashed dishes and the general mess in the kitchen.

"She went out early this morning. She's having problems with the bank," Tracy confided hesitantly. "Her bank manager wanted to meet her today to try to sort things out."

"Should I fill a bucket and wash this floor?" James suggested helpfully.

"Yes, please. There's one in that closet," Tracy said, pointing. She had stopped crying, Mandy saw with relief. "Mandy," she asked, "would you pick up the dirty newspaper and throw it in the trash for me? I'll go and start making the milk formula."

When Tracy had gone out of the kitchen, Mandy turned to James. "No mother dogs!" she hissed. "That's awful. People are coming here and buying these puppies without having seen them with their mother."

"Where do you think she's getting all the puppies from, then, if there are no mother dogs here?" James sounded puzzled.

"I don't know," Mandy told him, frowning. "But I know my mom and dad wouldn't like it. You're supposed to see pups with their mother when you buy one."

Mandy stepped gently over the barricade and three plump little puppies shuffled out of her way. In the box, some of the pups were still asleep, snuggled up tightly together with their legs intertwined, so that it was difficult to tell where one pup ended and another began. Mandy longed to pick them up and play with them but, somehow, these puppies didn't seem very interested in playing.

"She's really upset, isn't she? Tracy, I mean," James observed, dipping his mop into a bucket. "We'd better not ask her any more questions. She might get upset again."

"Hmm," said Mandy, torn between her anger about the motherless puppies and her sympathy for Tracy. "She said she had to give up college to help her mom out," she remembered. "I wonder what happened so that her mom couldn't cope?"

"It does sound strange," James agreed. Mandy had heaped the soiled newspapers into a pile, clearing an area of floor space for James's mop. The puppies had retreated into the big cardboard box and sat staring out with nervous expressions on their tiny faces.

"Oh, look at them, James!" Mandy sighed, getting down on her knees to look. "Aren't they great?" An assortment of blue and black eyes looked back solemnly at her. "I wish I could have one," she confessed.

The kitchen door squeaked as Tracy came back in carrying two large cans of a puppy milk formula. "This is Tina," she announced, as she put the cans down on the counter. "She's been snoozing in the sun, haven't you, darling?" Mandy looked up at a very large Old English sheepdog standing at Tracy's side. She had a bright orange beard of hair around her muzzle and her shaggy coat was a pale gray-blue color.

"Oh! Hello!" Mandy said to the dog, which towered over her as she kneeled on the floor.

"She's my mom's special dog," Tracy said. "She's had quite a few litters in her time. She's a wonderful mom." James rested the mop in the bucket and went forward with Mandy to pet Tina.

Tracy began measuring the milk powder into a bowl. "Tina and Troy were show dogs. My mother doesn't show any longer, so they have a quieter life now, really." Tracy poured warm water from a kettle into a measuring cup.

"They must need a lot of grooming," James said, running his fingers through Tina's thick coat.

"We comb them out about once a week," Tracy said, pouring the water onto the milk powder. "They need regular grooming, or their coats can get very tangled and matted."

James started mopping the floor. The puppies scampered away into their box, and peeped nervously out from the hole. Mandy watched Tracy making up milk for three bottles. "These feeding bottles are used for premature babies," Tracy told her, as she whisked the milk into a froth.

"Doesn't Tina feed any of the puppies herself?" Mandy asked, puzzled.

"None of these are Tina's pups," Tracy explained. "The last of her litter had been sold when these came to us. They're all Old English pups but different ages and from different litters."

Mandy tried not to look horrified. "Can I feed one of them?" she asked.

"I'll help!" James called. "I've finished doing the floor."

"All right," Tracy agreed. She screwed the tops onto the bottles and handed one to Mandy. It was warm. "You get started with these. They're for the three very small, dark-colored pups asleep in the box. I'll make up the food for the older ones." She smiled suddenly. "Thanks for helping," she said.

"We love helping animals, don't we, James?" Mandy said.

James nodded and held out an eager hand for the bottle.

Mandy sat cross-legged on the floor in the clean enclosure, with James beside her. She lifted a puppy onto her lap. It whimpered in protest at having been dis-

turbed from a warm and cozy sleep. Mandy stroked the pup's wrinkled little brow and held the bottle to its mouth. The puppy's nose twitched, then, with its eyes still closed, it grabbed it and began to drink. James reached into the big box and gently lifted another puppy.

"Wow," said James, surprised at the little dog's strength as it began to suck. "How old are these puppies, Tracy?"

"Not sure . . ." Tracy replied vaguely. "Those are

about four or five weeks, I think. Some are older."
James looked across at Mandy, who was frowning angrily. She knew that puppies weren't supposed to leave
their mother until they were at least six weeks old.
Surely any breeder ought to know that, too.

"They're so cute," James said quickly. "Mine's a girl.
What's yours, Mandy?" Mandy looked down at the
puppy in her lap. It was lying on its back, and pedaling
in the air with its front paws, concentrating on drinking
up the warm milk as fast as possible. "Um, let's see . . .
it's a boy!" she said.

Tracy was carrying over a series of shallow dishes
brimming with minced meat and puppy meal. "The big-
ger pups are on four meals a day," she told them with a
small shake of her head. "Feeding and cleaning up, then
feeding again . . . it never ends."

The puppy in Mandy's lap had finished his bottle and
was sitting on the floor, licking his lips. He looked up at
Mandy with sad dark eyes. She stroked him softly, mur-
muring, "Good boy." The puppy took a wobbly step
toward her and climbed over her legs, curling up in the
warmth and safety of her lap. He sighed and blinked up
at Mandy. Mandy ruffled the silky little head and
breathed in the smell of puppy and warm, sweet milk.

"You are a little sweetie," she whispered. The puppy
closed his eyes. Mandy wondered where his mother was.

She looked up at Tracy. "Did the mothers of all of these puppies die?" she asked sadly.

Tracy was laying out the puppies' dishes on the floor of the enclosure. As the puppies tumbled forward, eager for food, she separated them into groups of three and encouraged them by pressing on their noses.

"I don't know," Tracy replied absently. "We've never seen the mothers. They came to us to be sold. My mother agreed to take on one litter as a favor, and we've had nothing but trouble since!"

"Trouble?" Mandy asked, taking the second bottle of milk Tracy offered her. "What kind of trouble?"

James was frowning at Mandy. "My puppy has gone to sleep!" he announced, trying to change the subject. "Do you want to feed the third one, Mandy?" But Mandy only nodded.

"We've been overwhelmed by puppies needing homes," Tracy confessed, tucking her curly hair behind her ears. "Mom's been selling them at less than half the usual price, and it's costing us a fortune to take care of them all." She sighed angrily and plucked a greedy puppy out of its dish. Then she groaned as it began to track some gooey meat and meal across the floor.

"I really want to get back to college — but I can't," Tracy went on. "Mom can't cope on her own — not with this bunch!"

Mandy thought Tracy was going to cry again, so she said quickly, "Well, that's those two full of milk. Any more?"

"No more." Tracy shook her head. "But we'll need to put down fresh newspaper in a hurry or they'll begin to make a mess on the floor."

James leaped to his feet. "Right!" he said. "I'll get some. Where do you keep it?"

"Bottom of the broom closet," Tracy told him. "Thanks."

"I can fluff up the cushions in the box," Mandy suggested.

"If you like." Tracy smiled. Mandy waited while James spread newspapers on the floor, then, very gently, she lifted each of the puppies in turn out of the box. They huddled together on the floor, looking bewildered. Mandy untied the lace on one of her sneakers and dangled it in front of the pups. One crept forward to investigate but Mandy couldn't persuade him to play.

Eventually, Mandy gave up. She shook out the large cushion in the box, and plumped up the smaller ones. Then she put the younger puppies back into their bed. They snuggled together, making little mewling sounds.

James sighed as he spotted a fresh puddle spreading across the clean newspapers. "Phew! I see what you mean. It *is* hard work." He looked at his watch. "Mandy, we ought to go home now."

"Yes." Mandy stroked each of the pups in turn. "We'd better." She glanced at Tracy, who seemed cheerful enough now. She was eating an apple and smiling.

"So which puppy do you want to buy?" she asked. Mandy looked at James in horror, trying to remember exactly what she had said to Tracy earlier that morning.

"Um . . . how much are they?" James said.

"Three hundred each," Tracy said, "but my mom might give you a discount."

"Oh, that's far more than we could afford to spend," Mandy said quickly. "I'm sorry. I hadn't realized they would be so expensive."

"Purebreds are always expensive," Tracy pointed out.

"We'll have to save up," James shrugged. "Thanks for letting us play with them."

"Thanks for your help. I wish you could come every day," Tracy sighed.

"We could come again," Mandy offered at once. "It's school vacation now. We've got plenty of time. *Can* we come again?"

"Of course!" Tracy laughed. "If you don't mind working! Come on, I'll show you out."

Eight

"What a strange way to make money," James mused, strapping on his helmet. "I mean, it's like Mrs. Merrick has a production line of puppies. Someone keeps churning them out and passing them on to her to sell. It's cruel."

"It's terrible," Mandy said heatedly, picking up her bike and following James out through the dog's head gates. "How could anyone take those tiny puppies away from their mothers? We've got to do something to stop it." She shook her hair out of its ponytail. She was hot from the work and the cool breeze outside felt good.

"That girl — Tracy — didn't want to tell us much."

89

James looked at Mandy. "You nearly gave us away, asking all those questions!"

"I did not!" she answered indignantly. Mandy checked right and left, then pedaled out across the road to start the hilly two-mile ride back to Welford. James caught up to her on the opposite side.

"Sorry," he said, glancing at her.

Mandy grinned at him. Then she frowned. "James, look . . ." She braked and James followed her gaze back toward the bungalow. A white van had pulled onto the pavement outside Mrs. Merrick's gates. A man got out, walked around to the back, and unlocked the door.

"A delivery man," James said. "So what?"

"Don't make it so obvious that you're looking!" Mandy hissed. One half of the double door was open now; Mandy heard a sound like muffled yapping. "Can't you hear that noise? It sounds like puppies!" she whispered.

"Are you sure?" James asked.

"Come on." Mandy was impatient. "Let's double back and take a closer look, quickly, before he closes the door." Mandy pulled out back across the road.

"Hang on . . ." James called, following her. "I don't think . . ."

"Shh, James," Mandy pleaded. "Listen!"

They rode back toward the van. The driver was absorbed in his task. Bending from the waist, he seemed to be rearranging whatever was inside. As Mandy drew closer, she distinctly heard the sound of something whimpering.

Mandy stood at the back of the van. "Good morning!" she called brightly. The man straightened up so quickly that he hit his head on the roof of the van.

"Ouch!" He looked around, frowning. Seeing Mandy and James just behind him, he hastily slammed the door of the van. "What do you want?" he snarled.

"Um, can you tell us the way to Welford, please?" Mandy was listening for the noises from the van, hoping that James would hear them, too. But the whimpering noises had stopped.

"That way," the man growled, gesturing toward the main road. "Left."

"Oh, yes . . . thank you." Mandy smiled. The driver opened Mrs. Merrick's gates, then got back into the van. He started the engine and turned into the driveway.

"James!" Mandy whispered urgently. "He must be delivering the puppies."

"We don't know that, Mandy." James was doubtful. "You know what your mom said . . ."

"But we've got to do something! I heard puppies crying in the back of the van. Come on!"

"We could get ourselves into big trouble," James warned her. "And anyway, what are we going to do about it? Ask her to stop selling puppies?"

"There's something that's not right, James. You said so yourself!" Mandy insisted. "We'll bike on past for a little, then hide our bikes and sneak back. Okay?"

James shrugged and nodded.

They propped their bikes against the trunk of a tree in a leafy thicket set back from the pavement. Then, hurrying back toward the bungalow, they took cover among the leafy lower branches of a big elm growing by the entrance to the driveway.

"There!" Mandy whispered to James. "We've got a great view from here. Let's see what happens now." James didn't answer. He was crouched close to the trunk, peering out toward the driveway.

The man was leaning on the roof of the van, writing something in a little notebook. When he had finished, he put his pen in his top pocket, leaned inside the van, and honked the horn, making Mandy jump.

Beep! Beep! Beep!

James covered his ears. "Why can't he just go and ring the doorbell like everyone else?" he muttered.

Mandy watched as the front door opened. Tracy put her head out, then leaned out to see who was in the driveway. The man waved at her and walked forward.

"Hello," he called. "Is your mother in?" Mandy saw that Tracy was scowling as she walked toward the van. She was barefoot now, her arms folded across her chest. She tossed her bushy hair out of her face.

"She's out," Tracy said abruptly, her expression furious.

"That's a shame." He grinned. "I'll leave the dogs with you then, okay?" he said.

Mandy nudged James in the ribs. "Dogs!" she hissed. "Did you hear?" James's eyes were wide with horror.

"More puppies?" Tracy said, looking angrily at the man. "I thought my mother told you last time, we can't take any more. I'm not taking them."

"Ah, there must be a misunderstanding," the man replied smoothly. "I've got a lovely litter of Old English pups with me — real little champions in the making," he wheedled. "I can't take them anywhere else. I'm going to have to leave them here for your mother."

"No!" Tracy cried angrily.

"She's brave," James muttered. "I don't like the looks of him."

"I don't understand. Why are they taking dogs they don't want?" Mandy whispered. "What should we do?"

"We can't do anything at the moment." James was firm. "Let's stay here and watch. I'm going to memorize his license plate." James shuffled forward. The man was whistling as he walked back to the van. Mandy and James shrank back into the branches out of sight.

As soon as he began to rummage around in the van, Mandy pressed forward again to try to get a glimpse of the inside. It was too dark to see clearly, but she could hear the pitiful little yaps of the puppies.

"Make sure you tell your mother she's doing these pups a very good deed by taking them in, won't you," the man said, smiling at Tracy. "And I'll be back tomorrow for the money she owes me." He pulled a small wire cage from the van, swinging it alarmingly as he did so. Three tiny Old English sheepdog puppies slid around inside, yelping as they tried to stay upright.

"No!" Mandy gasped, outraged.

"Shh!" James warned.

"We can't take them, Mr. Evans," Tracy said calmly. "We don't have room for any more puppies and we can't sell them. We've got too many already. My mother said . . ."

"Now, you listen to *me*, girlie," the van driver said in a threatening tone. "I'm leaving these here for you, is that clear? And I'll be back for my money tomorrow." He put the cage down heavily on the driveway. Mandy saw the puppies flinch and cower as it clattered down.

"This is crazy!" Tracy shouted. "You just can't do

this!" But Mr. Evans had climbed back into his van, whistling, and started to rev his engine. He swung the van around noisily and turned out of the driveway, then accelerated away down the road.

Mandy stared at James. "Poor Tracy! We've got to help." She went to stand up, but James put out a hand to stop her.

"Not now. We don't want Tracy to know we've been spying on her, do we?" he said. "Let's get back to Animal Ark and tell your mom and dad."

Mandy looked out miserably from the cover of the tree. She saw Tracy slowly stoop to lift the little cage and hold it up to her face, peering in at the small bundles of white-and-black fur inside.

"Poor little things," they heard Tracy say. "Come inside and I'll feed you." She sighed deeply, then, closing the gates, she walked wearily up the driveway to the front door.

Mandy and James arrived back in Welford late in the afternoon, and pulled up at the town green.

"I'll come by with Jenny later, to find out what your mom and dad said," James told Mandy as he rode off toward home. Mandy turned down the lane toward Animal Ark.

In the living room, Dr. Adam and Dr. Emily were reading the Sunday papers. "Here you are!" exclaimed Dr. Emily, as Mandy burst into the room.

"We wondered where you were," her dad teased.

But Mandy was bursting with the news. "I didn't mean to be out so long, but we had to help Tracy with the puppies, and then a man tried to make her take some more . . ."

"Whoa!" said Dr. Adam, looking perplexed. "Stop, Mandy. Take a deep breath, and start from the beginning. Tracy who?"

Mandy sighed. "Well . . ." she began. "Mrs. Merrick wasn't at home but her daughter, Tracy, let us into the house to see the puppies. Only the puppies aren't okay, they don't want to play. There are twelve of them, all Old English sheepdogs, all from different litters . . ."

"So," Dr. Emily said carefully, "Mrs. Merrick keeps more than one mother dog in the house?"

"No!" Mandy exclaimed. "None of these puppies were Tina's — that's the dog she breeds from. Tracy wouldn't tell us how they got them all, but she said that her mom had taken some as a favor and it had caused nothing but trouble."

"How old would you say the pups were?" Dr. Adam asked.

"All different ages. Some were about eight weeks old, but there were some really tiny ones. Tracy said they were only four or five weeks old. James and I fed them with a bottle," Mandy added.

Dr. Emily looked across at her husband and raised her eyebrows. "Go on, sweetheart," she said quietly.

"James and I were just leaving," Mandy said, "when we saw a man arriving in a van. We hid in the trees, and we heard him try to make Tracy take some more Old English sheepdog puppies, but she wouldn't. So he just left them and drove off!" Mandy blinked as tears pricked her eyes. Dr. Emily got up and sat on the arm of her chair. She put an arm around Mandy's shoulders.

"He said Mrs. Merrick owed him money," Mandy added.

"Oh, dear. It sounds like a mess," Dr. Emily said.

"What can we do, Dad?" Mandy pleaded.

"Strictly speaking, this is none of our business." Her father was frowning. "Mrs. Merrick isn't even one of my clients, so I really can't interfere."

"But Ted Forrester could," Dr. Emily suggested.

"James has the license plate number of the van," Mandy said. "He's coming over later."

"That was good thinking." Dr. Adam grinned. "When he comes I'll give Ted a call and see if he knows anything about this van driver. If he's trading in puppies, he might be known to the SPCA."

"Why can't we go straight to the police?" Mandy asked.

"What for, Mandy? We don't know that a crime has been committed," her father explained. "All we know is what you have seen."

"Did Tracy Merrick know anything about the puppy you found?" Dr. Emily asked.

"Oh, yes!" Mandy replied. "She's one of their pups. She ran away! Tracy calls her Petal," she added.

"Well, that's good news," Dr. Adam said. "That gives us a reason to call Mrs. Merrick, doesn't it, Emily?"

"It does," she agreed.

"Now?" Mandy asked hopefully.

"Not on a Sunday evening, no," Dr. Adam told her. "It'll wait until tomorrow."

"But, Dad," Mandy said sadly. "You won't let Puddles — Petal — go back there, will you? It sounds like they're so desperate to sell the puppies that Petal could end up with anyone!"

Dr. Adam shook his head. "She belongs to Mrs. Merrick, Mandy," he reminded her.

"We'll just have to wait, Mandy," Dr. Emily said. "Dad is going to talk to Ted." She stood up. "I'm going to start dinner. Why don't you give me a hand."

Mandy was washing lettuce at the kitchen sink when James and Jenny knocked at the kitchen door.

"Hi," Mandy said. "Come in." Jenny looked serious.

"James told me all about your day. Those poor puppies!" she said.

Mandy nodded. "Did you bring that number, James?" she asked.

James rummaged in the pocket of his jeans and took out a scrap of paper. "Yup," he said. "Here it is."

"I'll just go and give it to Dad," Mandy said, running off to the living room to find him.

When she returned, Jenny and James were sitting at the kitchen table. James looked gloomy.

"Cheer up, James," said Dr. Emily. "Why don't you get everyone a cold drink. There's a jug of orange juice in the fridge."

"Ted's not around at the moment," said Dr. Adam, coming into the kitchen. "Oh, hello, Jenny. Hi, James." He joined them at the kitchen table. "He's off at some meeting in the Lake District," Dr. Adam continued. "But I've left a message — including the license plate number of the van. Well done, James."

"I'll get those drinks," James mumbled and went over to get some glasses from the cabinet.

Mandy stood up and took the orange juice from the fridge. "I just wish there was something we could do," she muttered.

"I know," Jenny exclaimed. "Why doesn't Mrs. Merrick take her puppies down to the pet shop in Welford? I bet they'd sell them for her."

Dr. Adam shook his head. "That's not quite what we would hope for the puppies, you see, Jenny," he explained. "We want to be sure they go to the right sort of home." Jenny looked disappointed, and Dr. Adam went on. "The first rule of buying a puppy is to see it with the mother dog. That way you can be sure that the puppies you see have had the right start in life. There are people who breed dogs just to make money. That means the mother dogs are kept in cramped, dirty, and often unsuitable conditions. And soon after their puppies are born, they are taken away to be sold."

"But why can't they leave the puppies with the mother until they are old enough to leave her?" Jenny asked, horrified.

"Because tiny puppies are much more attractive. They can be sold more easily," he replied, sighing.

"And, as soon as one litter of pups has been taken away, the mother dog is encouraged to breed another litter — until she is absolutely exhausted," Dr. Adam added, leaning over to put a large bowl of salad on the table.

"That's awful," Jenny said.

"Yes, it is," Mandy agreed dismally.

"The worst thing about this business," Dr. Adam went on, "is that the puppies are taken long distances from the farms where they are bred. They get put into a van with other puppies, from other mothers, without having had their vaccinations, so infections are easily spread. By the time they get to a pet shop, they can be in a pretty bad state."

"But why don't the police do something to stop it?" James asked.

"The law on breeding dogs is hard to enforce," Dr. Adam said sadly. "There's not much they can do unless there are obvious signs of cruelty — which there aren't in this case." A heavy silence fell around the table.

"Well," James said at last, "we'd better be getting back for our dinner." He looked at Jenny. She nodded and stood up.

Mandy smiled. "See you tomorrow?" she asked James and Jenny. "We'll meet here?"

"Yup," said James. "Tomorrow. I'll ask John if he wants to come, too. Bye."

When the door had closed Mandy slumped back into the chair.

"Why don't you go and see the puppy in the residential unit?" Dr. Emily suggested. "I bet she'd love a cuddle."

Mandy brightened. "Is there time before dinner?" she asked.

Dr. Emily nodded. "Just about. Don't be too long," she added with a smile.

*   *   *

"Hello, Puddles!" Mandy called softly. She wasn't used to thinking of the puppy as "Petal" yet.

Puddles turned and pricked up her small ears. She put her front feet on the door of her kennel and tried to lick Mandy's hands through the wire. Her little stump of a tail wagged with excitement.

"She seems brighter today," said Dr. Adam, who had followed Mandy into the unit to check on the patients. He lifted the puppy gently and looked at her gums and the rims of her eyes. Then he handed her to Mandy. "She's recovering quickly."

Puddles squirmed happily for a few seconds, licking at Mandy's hands. Mandy smoothed the puppy's silky head. Soon, Puddles climbed into Mandy's arms and sighed, her black button nose buried in the crook of Mandy's elbow.

"You're tired." Mandy chuckled. She held Puddles for a few more minutes, stroking her gently, then put her back into the kennel. The puppy made herself comfortable on the fleece lining, curling herself into a ball. She blinked sleepy eyes at Mandy.

"Poor Puddles," Mandy whispered. "Dad, what will happen to her if she has to go back to Mrs. Merrick?"

"We'll just have to wait and see," said her dad. "Now, let's go and have dinner."

Nine

The next day, Mandy slept later than usual and arrived in the kitchen just as her mother was pulling on her white coat, ready for the morning clinic.

"Good morning, honey." Dr. Emily smiled. "I'm just about ready. Dad's been called out to help at a calving." She tied her red hair back in a ponytail and picked up a pile of papers from the kitchen table. "What are you and James going to do with yourselves today?" she asked.

"Tracy Merrick said yesterday that we could help her with the puppies," Mandy told her. "I just hope that man doesn't come back and start bothering her again . . ."

Mandy felt a flush of anger, remembering the way Mr. Evans had bullied Tracy the day before.

"Well, make sure you keep out of it if he does," Dr. Emily said. "Just stick to helping out with the puppies."

"Okay." Mandy grinned, bending to lace up her sneaker. "But I'm going to visit our own special puppy first. I want to say hello to Puddles."

"Well, don't forget to have breakfast, will you?" Dr. Emily called, as she went out into the clinic.

In the residential unit, Simon, the veterinary nurse, was giving Puddles her breakfast. He looked up as Mandy came in. "Hi, Mandy. She enjoys her food, doesn't she?" he said.

Mandy laughed. "Yes, there's nothing wrong with her appetite now." The bridge of the puppy's nose was smeared with puppy food. Mandy kneeled beside her on the floor. "Slowly," she told the puppy, gently ruffling her head. "You'll choke if you eat it like that."

At the sound of her voice, Puddles paused and looked up. Mandy stroked the little pup and earned a messy lick. "Yuck." She giggled. "You've covered me in gravy now."

There was a knock at the door and Jean Knox appeared. "Mandy? James is in the waiting room — he's looking for you," she called.

"Okay. Thanks, Jean," Mandy said, getting to her feet. "I'm coming. Bye, Puddles. I'll come and see you later."

It was only just after nine, and already the waiting room was filled with animals and their owners. Mandy saw James, Jenny, and John waiting for her near the door. Dr. Emily was looking at a file of case notes behind the reception desk. She called Mandy over.

"I called Mrs. Merrick a while ago," she said. "I asked her what she wanted to do about the puppy."

Mandy's heart sank. "What did she say?" she asked anxiously.

"She explained that she had her hands full at the moment, so I suggested we keep Petal here — for the time being." Dr. Emily smiled as Mandy let out a sigh of relief. "Just remember, she will have to go back eventually," she warned.

"I know. Thanks, Mom." Mandy smiled. "We're going over there now. Okay?"

"Okay," Dr. Emily said. "But stay out of trouble, for goodness' sake."

"We will," Mandy said. "Promise."

There was a car parked in the driveway at the Merricks' house, and Mandy suddenly felt nervous. Mrs. Merrick must be home. What if she realized that she was being spied on?

"Here we are," James said, as he unlatched the gate. They wheeled their bikes up the driveway and laid them on the grass. Mandy was about to knock at the door when it swung open.

"I saw you through the window!" Tracy smiled. "Oh, hello!" She looked from one face to another in surprise. "You've brought your friends . . ."

"We'd all like to help," Mandy explained. "That is, if you don't mind. We thought Troy and Tina might want a walk — and we could clean up the enclosure and feed the puppies . . ." Mandy trailed off as Mrs. Merrick appeared, frowning, at her daughter's shoulder.

"Who is it, Tracy?" Mrs. Merrick asked.

"This is Mandy, Mom," Tracy said. "Remember, I told you she was here yesterday. And this is James. They've come to help with the puppies, and they've brought their friends, too."

"I'm James Hunter," James said politely, "and this is my cousin Jenny Thomas, and this is John Hardy."

"Well . . ." Mrs. Merrick looked flustered. "It's very kind of you, I'm sure, but . . ."

"Come in," Tracy interrupted her mother. "I could do with the help, and the puppies loved having you to play with."

Mandy saw Mrs. Merrick's steely face soften. She looked tired. There were shadows the color of bruises around her soft gray eyes and lines of worry on her forehead.

"We love dogs," Mandy explained. "We'd really like to see the puppies again." She looked up into Mrs. Merrick's face and gave what she hoped was a winning smile. Mrs. Merrick looked tense. Mandy held her breath.

"Come into the kitchen," Mrs. Merrick said at last, standing back from the door. She led the way through the house. Troy and Tiny came to sniff at the legs of the visitors and Mandy stooped to pet them.

"We've brought you some good news," James told Tracy.

"That's right," said Mandy. "Puddles — um — Petal — is much better. She's put on weight and her stomach is better, too."

"Yes, isn't it good news! I talked to the vet at the clinic this morning," Mrs. Merrick said, her face relaxing. "Thank you so much for rescuing her," she added. "I was so worried about the poor thing. I shouldn't have left Tracy alone to cope with so many pups, but I really did have to go out to buy their food."

"Don't get upset, Mom," Tracy said briskly. "It was *my* fault, not yours. Let's just be glad Mandy and James found her."

Mandy climbed over the barrier to look at the puppies, followed by James and Jenny. "Oh, wow!" Jenny cried. "There are so many of them!" She reached out to pick up one of the smaller pups that was struggling to climb out of the box bed.

"We've got another three puppies now," Tracy said grimly. "It's gong to take forever to feed and groom them all."

"Well, let's get started then," Mandy said eagerly. "What do you want us to do?"

"They'll want their food first," Mrs. Merrick said, glancing at her watch. "Then perhaps you could help to clean their area."

"That's a good idea," Tracy said. "Let's take them all out into the yard. We can feed them out there and they can get some exercise at the same time. With five of us to watch them, there's no chance of them escaping."

"Oh, yes," Mrs. Merrick agreed, sounding relieved. "The fresh air will do them all good."

"This will be their first time outside." Tracy smiled. "So it will be an adventure for them. Come on, let's go."

They carried the pups outside, two at a time, with Troy and Tina following Mrs. Merrick out into the sunshine. The backyard was long and narrow, with a large beech tree at the end that gave plenty of shade. Mandy set her puppies down on the grass in the shade.

The younger pups lay on their stomachs, their small

legs splayed out, and moved their heads from side to side, sniffing at the unfamiliar environment. Some of the puppies began to whimper, and one started to howl pitifully.

"Oh, no!" Jenny said. "They really don't seem to like it out here!"

"They're just not used to it," Mrs. Merrick told them, raising her voice to make herself heard. "Sit down with them, all of you . . . that's it. Now, see how they are cuddling up to you? It makes them feel safer."

Mandy lay down on her side on the grass, her body curved protectively around two of the younger pups. The puppies began to settle down, nosing around in the grass beside her. But Mandy noticed that none of the pups seemed very adventurous.

Jenny was sitting cross-legged in the sun with one of the puppies in her lap. It cowered there, peering out uncertainly.

"Oh, they are wonderful," Jenny breathed. "Do you only sell Old English sheepdogs?" she asked Mrs. Merrick.

"Yes, I've had them for years. They're a wonderful breed." She smiled. "They're all born black-and-white, then, as they grow, their coats turn a silvery gray." She bent down to stroke one of the pups that had ventured up to inspect her shoe.

"Okay," said Tracy, easing a puppy off her lap. "I think I'll go and make up the food, now."

"Thanks, Tracy," Mrs. Merrick said. "But I'll do it, if you like."

"No, Mom," Tracy said firmly. "You sit down for a while and have a break. I'll be fine." Tracy stroked Troy's woolly head and headed back into the house. Tina ambled after her.

As they sat on the lawn enjoying the sunshine, some of the older puppies grew more inquisitive and began to wander. Mandy was just retrieving one of the older pups from a rose bed when Tracy appeared at the door. "Time for lunch," she called, walking toward them across the grass with a big bowl in each hand.

"Can you get the other bowl from the kitchen for me, Mandy?" she asked. "Oh, and bring the milk bottles, too, please . . ."

"I'll help you," said Mrs. Merrick, getting up. "Come on, Mandy." Mandy followed Mrs. Merrick up to the house. "It's very kind of you to help us like this, dear," she said as she collected the milk bottles. "You must tell me all about how you found Petal. We were so worried . . ."

Mrs. Merrick trailed off, distracted by a knock at the front door. Mandy saw her glance apprehensively toward the hallway. "Oh, no!" she muttered. "It's that awful man again." There was another knock, and she hurried out of the kitchen and into the hall. Mandy began to load the puppies' milk bottles onto a tray she found lying on the kitchen table.

"Good morning, Mrs. Merrick," she heard a man's voice say. "Good to see you again . . ." Mandy was sure she recognized the voice of the man who had delivered the puppies to Tracy the day before. She stood still and listened.

"Now, Mr. Evans," she heard Mrs. Merrick say in an

exasperated tone, "I thought I told you that I couldn't accept any more dogs. You had no business leaving those puppies with my daughter."

"I've come about the money," he said, ignoring her remark. "They're a hundred and fifty each. That's what you owe me." Mandy crept closer to the kitchen door and peered into the hallway. She saw the driver of the van. He was standing in the doorway with his arms folded across his chest, and one foot on the step inside the front door.

"I don't *want* any more puppies! Can't you understand? I'm not paying for them. You had no right to leave them here," Mrs. Merrick was saying.

"What I understand is that you owe me money," he smiled, but there was something threatening about the way he loomed over her.

Mandy was furious. The man was obviously trying to frighten Mrs. Merrick.

"We had a deal, lady," Evans snarled.

"No," Mrs. Merrick said firmly. "We had no deal. You persuaded me to take on the first litter as a favor. You said your cousin was sick and couldn't look after them — you didn't say anything about the rest of these puppies."

"I sold them to you for a good price," Evans argued. "They're worth four hundred at least."

"Yes," Mrs. Merrick sounded angry, "and I paid you for the second litter you brought me, and the third litter — but I won't pay for any more. I don't want them. I can't take any more dogs. There aren't enough buyers in the area and I can't find homes for them all. You *must* take them away or else . . ."

"Or else what?" he sneered, leaning farther forward in the doorway. Mandy drew back, hiding herself behind the kitchen door.

"I'll go to the police!" Mrs. Merrick told him triumphantly.

Evans roared with laughter. Mandy was shaking with rage. She was about to run out into the hall when she heard James's voice behind her. "Where are those bottles, Mandy? The puppies are hungry and . . ."

"Shh!" Mandy frantically gestured for him to be quiet. "Come and listen to this," she whispered.

"What?" James said. "What is it?"

"Listen!" Mandy urged.

"What are the police going to say about you buying and selling dogs without a proper license? That's what I want to know!" Evans laughed again, as though it were the best joke he'd ever heard. Mandy was about to spring forward, but James held her back.

"Don't, Mandy!" he whispered. Mandy hesitated. Mrs. Merrick needed some support. Mr. Evans's foot was still jammed in the doorway, stopping her from being able to close the door in his face.

"He's trying to make her pay for the puppies he brought yesterday," Mandy whispered to James. "She told him to take them back and he threatened her."

"Now, let's not be hasty here, shall we?" Mr. Evans was saying soothingly. "You've done these pups a big favor. What would've happened to them otherwise? Now, I've got another pair in the van today, as it happens. They're champs in the making . . ."

"No!" shouted Mrs. Merrick. "Absolutely not, do you hear me?"

"All right, all right, keep your hat on," he said. "It's a shame, though. If you don't take them, I can't be responsible for what happens to them . . ."

Mrs. Merrick's resolve crumbled when she heard Evans's threat. "Oh! You wouldn't," she said tearfully. "You wouldn't put them down, you can't . . ."

"Well, if you won't take the poor little things in . . . I mean, they've been in the back of the van all night long. They need feeding. I can't keep them much longer," he said, shrugging his shoulders.

"I'll take them!" Mrs. Merrick cried. "You can't just abandon them."

"Now, that's what I like to hear," Evans said, chuckling. "I'll want payment, though. I'll tell you what, you go and get me my money. I'll bring the puppies out of the van, all right?" Evans finally stepped back from the doorway and walked toward his van.

Mrs. Merrick turned. Mandy could see tears running down her cheeks. Mandy stepped out into the hall to meet her. "You *can't* let that man bully you," she pleaded. "Can't we get the police?"

Mrs. Merrick looked shocked. "No!" she said, sounding horrified. "I have to sort this out myself. The police wouldn't understand. This could ruin me. If it got out what I'd been doing . . . I don't know how I have managed to get so caught up in this dreadful business."

"What's wrong, Mom?" Tracy had come in through the kitchen. She looked at her mother, then at Mandy. "What's happened?" she demanded. "What's going on?"

"That man came again, and he's making your mom take another two puppies," Mandy replied angrily.

"Evans?" Tracy asked. Mrs. Merrick nodded miserably. "No!" Tracy was horrified. "No more, Mom!" she begged. "We can't look after any more."

Mrs. Merrick shook her head. "What can I do?" she asked helplessly. Tracy put her arm around her mother's shoulders and led her back into the kitchen. Mandy and James exchanged glances, unsure of what to do.

"Will you two go and help Jenny, please?" Tracy

asked them, taking charge. "I've left her and John alone with all the pups. I think you'd better bring them back inside." She turned to her mother. "Sit down, Mom," she urged. "Let's try and think what to do."

Mandy and James ran outside to where Jenny and John were trying to keep all the puppies in one place.

"Where did you all go?" Jenny asked, puzzled.

"Sorry," Mandy said. "That horrible man has come back — with more puppies."

"Oh, poor Mrs. Merrick," Jenny breathed.

"And poor puppies!" said Mandy grimly.

"We've got to take them back inside," James told Jenny, picking up a puppy in each arm.

They gently carried the puppies back inside to their enclosure in the kitchen.

"Can we give them their bottles?" Jenny asked. "They must be hungry."

"The milk might need warming again," James said. "We'd better ask first."

"I wonder if . . ." Mandy began, then stopped. She could hear shouting. It sounded as if Tracy was in trouble.

Ten

Mandy leaped over the puppy barricade and sprinted down the hall. The front door was wide open but there was no one in sight. She could hear angry voices coming from outside. James gave Mandy a little shove from behind.

"Come on!" he said. "Quick."

"Do you think we should?" Jenny asked anxiously.

But Mandy was determined. "We might be able to help," she said, heading for the door.

Mrs. Merrick was facing a furious Mr. Evans through the bars of the gates. Tracy was leaning against the gates, stopping him from opening them.

"You stay out of this, miss," Evans was snarling. "You don't want to get hurt, do you?"

"Let him come in, Tracy," Mrs. Merrick pleaded. "I'll pay for the puppies this time — but they must be the last. Is that clear?"

"Don't pay him, Mom! We can't afford it," Tracy shouted. "This is blackmail."

Mandy's heart was hammering. She and James raced down the driveway to Mrs. Merrick with John and Jenny following them.

"Just give me the money you owe me for yesterday's puppies, and for these two I've got here," Evans said, kicking the cage by his feet. The two puppies whined. "Then, I'll go — and you can give these two a nice drink of water. They haven't had a drink for a long time." Mandy gasped in horror. It was such a hot day — had Evans really had those puppies in his van all morning without water?

Tracy, however, was obviously determined not to give in. "Just take your puppies and go!" she shouted. "Leave us alone."

Evans picked up the wire cage with the puppies. "Well, it looks like nobody wants you," he said, letting the cage fall to the ground with a clatter.

"No!" cried Mandy.

The puppies yelped in distress and Mrs. Merrick

could stand it no longer. "Let him *in*, Tracy," she commanded. "Those puppies are terrified. Let him have the money — as long as he'll go!" Tracy was beaten. She stepped aside. Evans pushed the gates open at once and stooped to pick up the puppies. He handed the cage to Mrs. Merrick.

"There, now you're being sensible." He smiled. "Just give me my money, and I'll be off." Mrs. Merrick murmured something soothing to the puppies and put them gently on the grass in the shade of a tree.

Evans was hovering close behind her. "My money . . ." he repeated.

Mandy was trembling with anger and frustration. Surely there must be something they could do? Then, suddenly, she spotted the keys to Evans's van dangling from the lock of the double doors at the back. She nudged James and nodded at where the keys hung, glinting in the sun. James gave a small nod.

As Steve Evans followed Mrs. Merrick toward the front door, Mandy slipped out of the gate. She plucked the keys from the lock and darted back onto the driveway, passing the keys to James, who put them in the pocket of his jeans.

"Thank you very much," Evans chuckled, as he counted his money. "I'll be on my way now."

"Don't come back," Tracy called as he strode out of

the gates toward his van. He went to close the back
doors and, finding the keys missing, checked inside the
driver's door. Mandy and James watched as he felt in
his pockets.

"My keys," he said. "The keys to my van . . . Where
are they?"

Mandy gazed back at him innocently, wondering how
she was going to get inside to call the police. James
shrugged.

"You'd better not be playing games with me," Evans
growled. He looked on the floor of the van.

"Tracy," Mrs. Merrick said, "let's take these puppies
inside and get them some water." She lifted the cage,
then paused as they heard the noise of an engine. A Land
Rover turned in the driveway and pulled up alongside
Evans's van.

"James, look," Mandy whispered. "It's Ted Forrester."

"Just in time," James sighed, running to the gate.

"Ted!" Mandy called, as the SPCA inspector got out
and walked up the driveway.

Ted Forrester looked puzzled. "Hello, you two," he
said. "I wasn't expecting to see you here. Hello, Mrs.
Merrick."

Mrs. Merrick looked confused, but Mandy pointed
toward the van. Evans had disappeared from view. Ted

walked over to the van and rapped on the passenger window.

"Mr. Evans, isn't it?" he called. "I notice your van's open at the back. Do you mind if I take a look inside?" The driver's door opened and Evans jumped out.

"Yes, I do mind," he protested. "It's none of your business what I've got in my van," he said, his lip curling. *Evans doesn't look so confident now*, Mandy thought, noticing the sweat running down his face. Ted walked calmly around to the back of the van. He gave a long, low whistle.

"And what have we here!" he said. "Puppies . . . Yorkshire terriers, a springer spaniel . . . Very hot in this van for dogs, Mr. Evans. I can't allow this, you know. It's causing unnecessary suffering, and that means I shall have to impound these dogs."

"You've got nothing on me," Evans sneered. "These dogs are my property and you can just leave them alone."

Ted looked unconcerned. "Perhaps you'd like to complain to the police?" He gestured to the police car that had just pulled up behind the Land Rover. "I'm sure they'll be pleased to sort this out for us . . ."

Mrs. Merrick had been watching in disbelief. Now she walked toward the van. "Mr. Forrester?" she asked meekly.

Ted smiled. "You remember me, don't you — we met at the Working Dog Trials a couple of years ago?"

Mrs. Merrick nodded silently. Tracy stepped up, carrying the cage with the two puppies. "These are *his* puppies," she said, pointing at Evans. "He's been forcing Mom to take them!"

"Has he now?" said Ted, turning back to Evans.

With his back up against the driver's door of his van, and no keys, Evans was cornered. He looked from Ted to Tracy and then back. Then, pushing past them both, he shoved Tracy out of the way as he headed back toward the driveway. "Ouch!" said Tracy, startled.

"Stop him!" yelled Mandy, as Evans hurled himself back through the gate.

James ran after him with Mandy hot on his heels.

Evans ran around the side of Mrs. Merrick's house, scrambling over a small wooden side gate. Mandy pressed the latch, opened the gate, and followed.

Evans burst around the corner of the house and began to run for the tree at the end of the yard.

"Mandy," James panted, "if he gets over the fence we've lost him! There are fields on the other side."

Suddenly, the yard was filled with the sound of angry barking. Troy, who had been dozing in the shade of a tree, had woken up and was now chasing the intruder across the grass. He rushed toward him and lunged for Evans's ankle. Mandy heard the sound of jeans ripping.

Evans lost his balance and fell with a thud, landing heavily on his shoulder. He lay on the grass, unable to get up. Troy stood over him, snarling threateningly as Mandy and James skidded to a halt beside him.

Ted arrived just behind them, with a police officer Mandy recognized as one of the Walton wildlife team.

Mr. Evans lay on the ground groaning, nursing his injured shoulder. The policeman crouched down and slipped a pair of handcuffs around Evans's wrists. "We've been talking to your friends in Wales, Mr. Evans, and we think you've got some explaining to do," he announced, as he helped Evans to his feet and led him back toward the police car.

James, who was bent over trying to catch his breath, looked up at Mandy and grinned. "We did it," he said.

"What will happen to Mr. Evans?" Mandy asked Ted Forrester. They were sitting around the table in Mrs. Merrick's kitchen. Tracy was pouring drinks while Jenny passed around some snacks.

"We'll prosecute him for causing unnecessary suffering," Ted said, taking a cup from Tracy. "And for breaking just about every other rule in the book. The SPCA

has been investigating a farm in Wales for a while —
now we have plenty of evidence."

"But how did you know he was here?" Mrs. Merrick
asked timidly. Her hand strayed to Troy's fluffy head. He
was lying peacefully at her feet.

"Well, it was young James's quick thinking," Ted explained, grinning.

"Mine?" said James, puzzled. "How?"

"You took down the license plate of the van. Dr.
Adam gave it to me and I passed it on to the Welford
police station," Ted explained. "We ran the number
through the computer and came up with the link to a
Welsh farm. And after what you told your dad, Mandy,
about Evans trying to intimidate Tracy, we thought we'd
better come up here right away."

"I can't believe how stupid I've been," Mrs. Merrick
sighed, shaking her head. "I should never have let myself get involved in such an awful business."

"How did you meet Steve Evans, Mrs. Merrick?" Ted
asked, taking a sip of his iced tea.

Mrs. Merrick sighed. "At a dog show in Harrogate. He
saw my dogs, Troy and Tina, and told me he had a
cousin in Wales whose Old English sheepdog had just
given birth. A litter of nine, he said."

"And he wanted you to take them?" asked Ted.

Mrs. Merrick nodded. "He said his cousin was sick

and couldn't keep the pups. He persuaded me to buy them. Tina didn't have a litter to care for, so he sold them to me at a reasonable price," she admitted.

"Mom gave him the money for the litter and we didn't expect to see him again," Tracy explained.

"Go on," said Ted.

Mrs. Merrick continued. "Well, then he came back. He brought another litter — six beautiful pups. I'd already sold two from the first litter, but I didn't want to take any more, and I couldn't understand how his cousin had another litter so soon." She sniffed. "And, of course, he wanted a lot more money for them."

"He told Mom he'd put the puppies down if she didn't take them," Tracy said angrily.

"I knew there was something suspicious about the way he kept turning up with these Old English sheepdogs. And I knew they had been taken from their mothers too young, but they were so tiny — and some weren't well looked after. I couldn't turn them away."

"Mom was too frightened to go to the police — or the SPCA," Tracy explained. "Evans had pointed out that she didn't have a license to buy and sell puppies. She was just trying to help, but he told her she had already broken the law."

Mrs. Merrick burst into tears. "I was terrified people might find out what I'd done," she confessed.

"But you were trying to help," Mandy cried. "It's not your fault."

"You looked after the puppies when no one else would," Jenny added.

"I suppose I'm in trouble with the police, too," Mrs. Merrick went on miserably.

Ted Forrester smiled. "I suspect that the police will be satisfied with catching Mr. Evans. Let's hope they can get you some of your money back."

Mrs. Merrick sighed with relief. "Mr. Forrester, we still have fourteen puppies. I don't suppose you know of anybody who could take one?"

"I think the best thing," Ted said, "is for the SPCA to take all the pups into our kennels. We'll find them good homes." He stood up. "Well, I'd better be off. Thanks for the iced tea." He looked at Mandy, James, John, and Jenny. "I think you ought to be getting home, too," he said.

Mandy grinned, and stood up to go.

"Um, Mr. Forrester . . ." James said. "What should I do with these?" He reached in his pocket and handed over the keys to Evans's van.

"I thought I told you to stay out of trouble!" exclaimed Dr. Emily, when Mandy had reported the events of the day.

"What a team," said Dr. Adam, shaking his head. "It was good thinking to take Evans's keys." He laughed at the thought of Evans desperately searching for his keys.

They were in the kitchen at Animal Ark. Dr. Emily had laid out a wonderful spread of sandwiches and fruit on the table for lunch.

"Troy was wonderful," Mandy told her mom. "You should have seen him bring Mr. Evans down!"

"We never gave Troy and Tina their walk," Jenny remembered, sounding rather disappointed.

"I've got a feeling you'll be seeing Mrs. Merrick and her dogs again before the end of your stay here, Jenny," Dr. Emily said, taking a sip of her drink. As she did so, the telephone rang. Dr. Emily got up to answer it.

"Hello? Oh, I see. Yes, just a minute please." Dr. Emily was smiling as she turned. "It's for you, Mandy. It's a reporter from the *Walton Gazette*."

Mandy leaped out of her chair and ran to take the receiver.

"Hello? This is Mandy Hope," she said. "The dog wash? Oh, yes. Yes, tomorrow will be fine. Thank you. Okay. Bye."

Mandy put down the phone.

"Well?" asked James excitedly.

"They want to interview us for an article about the

dog wash," Mandy announced, grinning. "And they want to take our pictures."

"Fame at last!" James exclaimed.

Dr. Adam stuck his head through the door. "Hey! Sherlock Holmes? Dr. Watson?" Mandy and James looked up.

"Oh, hi, Dad," Mandy said.

"Mrs. Merrick has just called the clinic. She and her daughter want to take Petal home tomorrow. She said they want to give her the best life they can to make up for the horrible start. I thought you'd like to know."

James looked at Mandy. "We can visit her there," he said.

"Yes," said Mandy. "I'm sure we can. And she'll have a wonderful life with Mrs. Merrick and Tracy." She took a bite of her sandwich. "It's all ended perfectly for our little puppy in a puddle after all."

TM

Look for the next
Animal Ark ™ *book:*

TABBY IN THE TUB

Mandy Hope and James Hunter cycled out of Welford village. Daffodils nodded in the spring sunshine as they passed. "I've got a biology test today," Mandy groaned. "I looked over it for two hours last night and I still haven't learned it."

Mandy knew that if she wanted to be a vet then she had to do well in school, but she hated studying for tests. There were always so many other things that she would rather be doing — like looking after the animals that came into Animal Ark, her parents' veterinary practice.

"You'll do fine," James, her best friend, reassured her. They approached the last row of houses. "Race you up the hill!" he called. Not waiting for Mandy's answer, he put his head down, his brown hair flopping over his face, and started to pedal like mad.

"That's not fair!" Mandy protested, pedaling furiously after him.

As James sped past the first house, Mandy's sharp eyes noticed a cat coming out of one of the cottage gates just ahead of him. It was a white Persian cat. A very pregnant, white Persian cat who was heading straight toward the road.

James's eyes were looking down as he tried to make the most of his head start.

"James!" Mandy yelled. "Look out!"

The cat stepped out, her head held high. Her large, cumbersome body swayed as she walked.

"Stop!" cried Mandy in horror.

At the very last moment, James saw the cat. He jammed on his brakes and his bike skewed violently to one side, missing the cat by inches.

James and the bike crashed to the ground.

Mandy screeched to a halt and flung her bike onto the pavement. She raced over to the cat and scooped her up. Was she all right? Were there any signs of shock? The cat's rough tongue flicked over Mandy's hand and she rubbed her head against Mandy's chin. She wasn't hurt, just rather surprised at having such an unexpected cuddle. "Oh, thank goodness!" Mandy whispered, hugging her close.

Suddenly she remembered James and looked across the road.

He was gingerly disentangling himself from his bike. "Are you all right?" Mandy asked, hurrying over.

"I think so," said James, pushing his glasses firmly back onto his nose. He looked anxiously at the cat in Mandy's arms. "How is she?"

"Okay, I think," Mandy said, stroking the cat's soft white fur. "It's Delilah. You know — she belongs to Mr. Ward."

James nodded and stroked the cat's head. Bill Ward was the village mailman. They often passed him doing his rounds on their way to school. "He brought her in to Animal Ark a couple of weeks ago for a checkup on her pregnancy," Mandy said. Delilah looked up at her and purred.

"When are her kittens due?" James asked, wheeling his bike off the road.

"In about two weeks, I think," said Mandy. She looked around at the row of pretty gray stone cottages that nestled together, with sloping roofs and tiny windows. "We can't leave her out here. Shall we see if Mrs. Ward is in?"

"Which house is it?" James asked.

Mandy nodded toward a cottage near the end of the row. "The one with the pink cherry tree in the yard."

Each of the cottages had a front yard bordered by a shrubbery hedge. James pushed open the wooden gate that led into the Wards' yard. The spring breeze sent fluffy pieces of pale-pink cherry blossom swirling around Mandy's head. Two terra-cotta pots stood by the front door, purple and white pansies spilling out of them. James reached the door and knocked loudly. A dog barked inside and they heard footsteps approaching.

"Back, Tara!" said a voice inside, and Jane Ward, the mailman's wife, opened the door. She was dressed in jeans and a sweatshirt. A black-and-tan dog, about the size of a small Labrador, attempted to wriggle past her but she caught its collar quickly. "Steady, Tara." As she caught sight of Delilah in Mandy's arms, her inquiring look changed to one of surprise. "Delilah! How did you get outside?"

"We found her crossing the road," Mandy explained.

"I almost ran her over," admitted James, rather shamefaced.

"But we think she's all right," said Mandy quickly, seeing a look of concern cross Mrs. Ward's face. "James didn't touch her."

"I must have forgotten to lock the cat-door flap,"

groaned Jane, running a hand through her curly blond hair. "Thank you so much for bringing her back in. I've been trying to keep her in the house — unless I'm outside — to keep an eye on her. Her road sense has been terrible since she got pregnant."

Tara, the dog, was still struggling to greet Mandy and James. Giving up the battle, Jane released her hold on the collar and Tara bounded out joyfully.

James grabbed her just in time to stop her from jumping up at Mandy and Delilah. "Whoa, Tara!" The dog licked his face and hands ecstatically. She was an Australian cattle dog, square-shaped, strong and sturdy, with a head a bit like a German shepherd's. James and Mandy had first met Tara when she was just a few months old, and the Wards had bought her to keep Delilah company. Her heavy tail thwacked against James's legs. "She's as lively as always!" said James with a grin.

Jane smiled and took Delilah from Mandy. "It's certainly quite a job keeping an eye on both of them." She put Delilah down and sighed as the cat stalked slowly toward the kitchen. "I don't know what I'm going to do with Delilah. She's never been good with traffic, but she's been ten times worse since she's been pregnant."

"Just like Duchess," said Mandy, remembering. "She got hit by a car when *she* was pregnant." Duchess was

Delilah's mother. The accident had caused her to go into premature labor — luckily both Duchess and all her kittens had survived. She belonged to Richard Tanner, one of Mandy and James's friends in the village. James let Tara go and the happy dog bounced over to Mandy to say hello. Mandy bent down to pet her and received a lick on the nose. Mandy grinned and scratched Tara's ears. "How are you going to like the kittens, Tara?"

Jane raised her eyebrows. "We hope she's going to get along fine with them, but we'll keep her away from them at first, at least until they're old enough to cope with her bounciness. We were going to ask your dad about the best way to introduce them. Bill's planning to bring Delilah to the clinic for another checkup tonight."

"Oh, good," said Mandy, straightening up and looking pleased. "I'll see her then."

Jane nodded. "And you must both come and see the kittens when they are born. It's good for kittens to have visitors." She smiled. "Anyway, I'd better let you two get off to school or you'll be late. Thanks again." She called to Tara. The dog bounded happily inside.

Mandy and James turned back down the path and the door shut behind them. "Well, that turned out all right," said James, relieved. "Now I've just got to see if my bike's still working."

Mandy nodded but she was only half listening. A slight movement in the hedge had caught her eye. What was it? It looked like an animal. She frowned.

"Earth to Mandy!" said James, waving a hand in front of her face.

Mandy brushed him away and stopped. "Look," she said, in a low voice. "Over there in the hedge. It's a cat."

James frowned. "Where? I can't see anything."

"There," Mandy insisted, pointing.

James peered at the hedge. A short-haired tabby cat was lying watching them. Her brown-and-black fur blended in perfectly with the shadows. Her ears twitched warily. Her sleek, round body was tense.

Mandy held out her hand and approached quietly. "Here, puss. There's a good cat." She wondered what the cat was doing in the Wards' yard and why it looked so nervous. The cat crouched even farther into the ground. Now that she was closer, Mandy could see that the cat's left ear was torn. Dark clots of dried blood were caked around the nasty wound. Mandy edged closer but it was too close for the cat. Leaping up, it raced across the grass and scrambled clumsily through the far hedge.